A RAC   ... PROMISE

BEATRICE WYNN

CHAPTER 1

Eliza Tate woke to darkness. The November cold bit through her thin blanket, seeping from the floorboards and walls of their third-floor room. She stayed still for a moment, listening to Harry's breathing, that troubling rattle still there but no worse than yesterday. The empty pallet in the corner told her what she already knew. Father hadn't come home.

She rose without sound, bare feet finding the cold floor. The embers in the small grate had died to nothing. She knelt and blew gently, adding the last splinter of kindling they owned. A tiny flame flickered, casting weak light across the cramped space they called home.

The room held little: three pallets on the floor, a

table with one leg shorter than the others, a single chair with a broken back, and a wooden crate that served as storage for what few possessions they owned. No luxuries. Nothing that couldn't be left behind when rent became impossible.

Eliza ran her fingers through her tangled hair, numbers running through her mind. Five shillings due to Mr. Finch by week's end. Two shillings needed for Harry's cough mixture. Food would take whatever remained.

She glanced at her brother's sleeping form. Ten years old but small enough to pass for seven, with skin stretched too tight across his cheekbones. He curled around himself for warmth, dark hair falling across his face.

"Harry," she whispered, touching his shoulder. "Time to wake."

He stirred, opening his eyes to reveal the same Tate blue as their father's, though without the clouded look drink had brought to Thomas Tate's gaze.

"I dreamed of cake," Harry murmured, sitting up. "With sugar on top."

Eliza smiled. "Perhaps for Christmas."

"Will Father be home for Christmas?"

"If he finds work." She kept her voice light, hiding

the doubt she felt. Thomas Tate hadn't held work since their mother died. Three years of watching him disappear into drink, one day at a time.

She moved to the wooden crate in the corner, pulling out the chipped bowl she'd found abandoned behind a restaurant. The porridge inside had congealed overnight, but she'd saved it precisely for this morning.

"Breakfast." She handed the bowl to Harry. "Eat slow. Make it last."

He nodded, using the bent spoon to take tiny bites. Eliza checked his forehead for fever with the back of her hand.

"I feel better today," Harry said. "I can come with you."

"You should rest."

"I want to help." His chin lifted in the stubborn way that marked him as her brother. "I know how to spot good cloth. I found that silk scrap last week."

"You did." She couldn't afford pride, but it filled her chest anyway. "Get dressed then. Quiet so we don't wake Mrs. Bell next door."

While Harry dressed, Eliza lifted the loose floorboard beneath her pallet. The hiding spot held her most valuable possession: a small tin containing two pennies. She'd been saving for months, one penny at a time when luck allowed. Someday the tin would hold enough for a used sewing machine. She'd seen one in a pawn shop window for fifteen shillings, a fortune for a ragpicker, but a path to something better.

She tucked the tin back in its place and pushed the board firmly down.

Harry appeared at her side, dressed in clothes too big and too worn, his coat missing buttons, his boots resoled with cardboard. But his face had been washed, his hair combed with his fingers.

"Ready?" she asked.

"Ready."

They descended the narrow stairs, past doors behind which families slept crowded together, sometimes eight or ten to a room. The building creaked around them because the walls were so thin everyone heard the arguments, crying babies, coughing elders and the sounds of Spitalfields waking to another day of scraping by.

Outside, fog hugged the ground, mixing with smoke from factory chimneys. The November sun remained hidden, leaving the street in gray half-light. It smelt of sewage and rot and too many bodies packed close.

"I hate that smell," he muttered.

"Think of it as job security," Eliza replied. "Where there's waste, there's work for ragpickers."

They walked east, toward streets where wealthier households discarded better quality refuse. Harry kept pace despite his shorter legs. They passed familiar faces: Mrs. Burrows setting up her match stall, Mr. Peavey sweeping the front of his tobacco shop, Blind Pete sitting on his usual corner with his tin cup.

"Morning, Miss Eliza," Mrs. Burrows called. A widow with hands gnarled from years making matches, her face bore sulfur burns, but her eyes remained kind. "Who's this strapping lad? Can't be little Harry."

"Morning, Mrs. Burrows." Eliza paused. "Harry's feeling better today."

"Strong as a horse," Harry declared, making the old woman laugh.

"I saved these for you." Mrs. Burrows held out two withered apples. "Found them behind the fruit seller's stall. Bruised but still good inside."

Eliza took the offering, knowing refusal would hurt more than acceptance. "Thank you. That's right decent of you."

"World's hard enough without being stingy," Mrs. Burrows replied. "You two watch yourselves today.

Heard the Bulls were out in force yesterday, checking for picking licenses."

Eliza nodded. Police constables -Bulls to the locals meant changing their route to less patrolled streets. Nobody cared if the poor collected garbage, except when someone decided to enforce ordinances requiring ragpicker licenses none of them could afford.

She tucked one apple in Harry's pocket, the other in her own. "For later," she told him. "When you need it most."

They continued through streets that grew narrower, buildings leaning toward each other overhead as if sharing secrets. Harry's eyes darted everywhere, trained to spot anything useful in the gutters.

"Look!" He pointed toward an alley. "Someone's tossed out a rug."

Eliza followed his gaze to a rolled carpet propped against a wall, its edges frayed. "Good eyes. If it's wool, Melvin might pay three pence for it."

They approached the rug cautiously, because finds this good often came with competition. Eliza unrolled one edge, checking the material.

"Wool," she confirmed. "And no bugs. Help me roll it proper."

They worked to make the carpet portable,

binding it with twine Eliza kept in her pocket for such discoveries. Harry carried one end, Eliza the other, as they made their way to the secondhand shops along Brick Lane.

Melvin's shop occupied a narrow storefront, its window displaying an odd assortment of used goods. The bell jangled as they entered. The smell of dust and old textiles greeted them.

Solomon Melvin looked up from his ledger, his spectacles perched on his nose. "Miss Tate. Master Harry. What treasure brings you here today?"

Eliza nodded toward the carpet. "Found it abandoned."

"Let's have a look." Melvin came around the counter, running practiced hands over the wool. "Moths got to one corner. Stain here. Smoke damage." He glanced up. "Three pence."

"It's six feet long at least," Eliza countered. "Good wool. Five pence."

"Four," Melvin said. "Final offer."

"Four," Eliza agreed. She'd expected as much.

Melvin counted coins into her palm, and she closed her fingers around them, the metal still warm from Melvin's pocket.

"Any other bits today?" Melvin asked.

"Day's just starting," Harry piped up. "We'll find more."

Melvin smiled at the boy. "No doubt. The Tates have the best eyes in Spitalfields." He reached beneath his counter. "Here. Daily paper from yesterday. For you, young man."

Harry took the newspaper with reverence. Reading material came rarely. Any words fed his hunger for learning.

"Thank you, Mr. Melvin." Harry tucked it carefully inside his jacket.

"You mind your sister now," Melvin said. "World gets tougher every day."

Outside, Harry bounced on his toes. "Four pence! And a newspaper!"

"A good start," Eliza agreed. "Let's try the lanes behind the cloth merchant houses. They sometimes toss cutting scraps."

They headed west toward the warehouses where merchants stored imported textiles. The streets grew cleaner, the buildings newer. People here wore clothes without patches, shoes without holes. They looked through ragpickers rather than at them, as if poverty might be catching.

Harry walked closer to Eliza's side, his shoulders hunching against the dismissive glances. She kept her own spine straight, eyes forward. She never looked down for these people, no matter how they looked at her.

Behind a row of merchant offices, they found the day's hunting grounds: refuse bins containing cloth scraps too small for the cutters but valuable to those who collected such things. Other ragpickers had come and gone already, but pickings remained for those willing to dig.

"You take that bin, I'll check this one," Eliza directed. "Remember "

"Silk and wool first, cotton second, linen if clean," Harry recited. "No stained pieces unless the stain might wash out."

"Smart lad." She ruffled his hair, then turned to her own search.

For two hours they sorted through cast-offs, building small piles of usable material. Eliza found herself humming their mother's old work song as she dug, a habit that surfaced when her hands stayed busy. She stopped when she realized Harry had gone still, watching her with a strange expression.

"What?" she asked.

"You sound like her when you do that," he said.

The comment hit like a fist to her chest. Sarah

Tate had been dead three years, but some moments brought her rushing back.

"Do I?" Eliza managed.

Harry nodded. "It's nice. I forget sometimes what she sounded like."

Eliza swallowed against the tightness in her throat. "She sang that song whenever she worked. Said it kept her fingers nimble."

"Father doesn't like when you hum it."

"Father doesn't like remembering," Eliza said. "Sometimes remembering hurts too much."

Harry considered this, then returned to his sorting. "I want to remember. Even the hurting parts."

Eliza watched him for a moment. This boy with an old soul, forced to understand too much, too young. She wanted to shield him from the world's hard edges but knew she couldn't. The best she could manage was to soften the blows when possible.

The church bells rang noon as they tied their collections into bundles. Eliza's shoulders ached from bending, but her spirits lifted at the decent haul they'd accumulated: wool scraps from fine suiting material, silk cuttings in jewel colors, even a length of ribbon someone had discarded for a small flaw in its weave.

"These will fetch a good price at Rosie's shop," she told Harry. "Maybe even a shilling if she's in a generous mood."

Harry's stomach growled loudly, making them both laugh.

"Time for those apples," Eliza decided.

They sat on a low wall outside a warehouse, munching the bruised fruit and watching workers load wagons with goods. Harry pulled out his newspaper, sounding out words with Eliza's help when needed. The comfortable ritual paused when voices raised nearby drew their attention.

Two men stood posting notices on the warehouse door. Their official armbands marked them as working for the parish council. A small crowd gathered to read what they'd posted.

"What's happening?" Harry asked.

"Stay here," Eliza told him, moving closer to see.

The notice, printed in stark black letters, announced rent increases for parish-owned tenements, including their building on Fern Street. Rates would rise by two shillings per month, effective the first of December.

Eliza felt cold spread through her chest. Two more shillings when they already scrambled for every penny. Impossible math.

A voice spoke beside her. "Bloody council wants blood from stones."

She turned to see Mr. Tucker from the floor beneath theirs, his face lined with the same worry she felt.

"When did they decide this?" she asked.

"Last night's meeting. Said repairs cost more than expected." Tucker spat on the ground. "What repairs? The place is falling down around our ears."

Eliza stared at the notice, willing the numbers to change. "Two shillings."

"Might as well be twenty for most of us," Tucker said. "Your father know yet?"

"He's not been home." No need to explain why. Everyone knew Thomas Tate's weakness.

Tucker's expression softened. "You tell him I heard the shipyard's hiring. Strong back's all they ask for."

"Thank you, Mr. Tucker. I'll tell him."

She returned to Harry, who watched her face with concern too keen for a child.

"Bad news?" he asked.

"Just changes," she replied. "Nothing we can't manage."

"You have that look when you're worried."

Eliza smiled despite herself. "Too smart for your

own good, you are." She helped him gather their bundles. "Come on. Let's see what Rosie will give us for these treasures."

They walked east again, toward a small shop tucked between a baker and a tobacconist. The painted sign above the door read "Rosie's Mending & Alterations" in faded letters. Inside, the shop smelled of steam and starch, with racks of clothing waiting for repair.

Rose Bennett looked up from her worktable, spectacles magnifying her sharp eyes. At sixty, her fingers remained nimble, and her reputation for quality work brought customers from beyond Spitalfields.

"Well, if it isn't my favorite suppliers," she greeted them. "What've you brought old Rosie today?"

Eliza unwrapped their bundles on the counter. "Best pickings from behind Morley's textile house."

Rosie's fingers moved through the scraps with expert assessment. "Good wool here. Silk's nice quality." She held up the ribbon. "This I can use today. Lady brought in a dress with torn trimming."

She continued her evaluation, separating the materials into piles. "Eight pence for the lot."

Eliza had hoped for more but knew Rosie's first offer usually stood. "Fair enough."

"And this." Rosie reached beneath her counter, producing a small package wrapped in brown paper. "Leftover meat pie from my lunch. Boy looks like he could use it."

Harry's eyes widened at the offering. Eliza hesitated only briefly before accepting.

"Thank you, Miss Bennett."

"Call me Rosie, child. Known you since you were knee-high." She counted coins into Eliza's hand. "Your mother was one of my best seamstresses. You've got her eye for quality."

"She taught me to recognize good material."

"She taught you more than that." Rosie's gaze turned shrewd. "I see how those fingers of yours twitch when you look at my needlework. You still practice?"

"When I can. Light's poor in our room." Eliza glanced at Harry, who had already unwrapped the pie and begun eating. "And thread costs money."

Rosie nodded. "Tell you what. You bring me good silk scraps like these, I'll save you my thread ends. Can't sell them, too short for proper work, but enough for practice."

"I'd be grateful," Eliza said, meaning it. The chance to keep her stitching skills sharp might someday lead to something more than ragpicking.

"Your mother had plans for you," Rosie continued. "Said you had the touch for fine work."

A lump formed in Eliza's throat. "That was before."

"Before don't matter. Skill's still in those hands." Rosie returned to her sewing machine. "You mind those coins now. Plenty would steal from a girl if given half a chance."

They left the shop with twelve pence total, eight from Rosie, four from Melvin. Almost enough for Harry's medicine but not enough for anything else. And with rent increasing…

The afternoon passed in similar fashion. They searched refuse piles, sorted the findings, and sold what they could to various shops. By dusk, they'd earned another six pence, which brought their total to eighteen for a full day's work. Not terrible, but not enough.

Harry's cough had returned as the day cooled, each hack making Eliza wince. She steered them homeward as darkness fell, knowing his strength had limits.

"Will Father be home?" Harry asked as they climbed the stairs to their room.

"We'll see," Eliza said, though she had little hope.

The room stood empty when they entered, the

grate cold. Eliza busied herself lighting their last candle, gathering scraps of coal from their meager supply, coaxing a small fire to life. Harry sat on his pallet.

"We did well today," Eliza said, counting their coins once more. "Eighteen pence. Almost enough for your medicine."

"Use it for rent," Harry argued. "My cough isn't bad."

"Your cough needs medicine." She tucked the coins into her pocket. "I'll find more tomorrow."

She prepared their simple supper: a crust of bread from yesterday, shared between them. Harry's portion included the last bite of cheese they owned.

After supper, Harry curled up with his newspaper while Eliza mended a tear in his shirt. The quiet moment felt almost peaceful until heavy footsteps sounded on the stairs, followed by the door crashing open.

Thomas Tate stood swaying in the doorway, his large frame filling the space. He was once handsome, but now his face had grown puffy from drink and his eyes was bloodshot. But beneath the dissipation, traces remained of the man who had once sung to his children and taught Harry to whittle.

"There they are," he slurred. "My little money-makers."

Eliza set aside her mending. "Evening, Father."

He stumbled into the room, dropping onto his pallet. "What treasures did you find today, then? Make your old father proud?"

"Eighteen pence," Eliza answered carefully. "Good haul."

Thomas extended his hand. "Let's have it then."

Eliza hesitated. "It's for Harry's medicine. And rent's gone up two shillings for December."

"Rent?" Thomas laughed, the sound harsh in the small room. "Don't you worry about rent. Your father's taken care of everything."

A cold feeling spread through Eliza's stomach. "What do you mean?"

"Made an arrangement with Mr. Lockwood. The gentleman who runs the workhouses." Thomas pulled a folded paper from his coat. "Gave me five shillings advance. Plenty for rent."

Eliza took the paper, dread building as she read the cramped handwriting. It outlined a loan agreement: five shillings now, seven to be repaid by month's end. Signed by Thomas Tate, witnessed by Silas Grady, Lockwood's notorious debt collector.

"You borrowed from Lockwood?" Her voice

emerged strangled. "Father, his interest is robbery. And if you can't pay…"

"I'll pay," Thomas insisted, his dignity attempting to push through the drunken haze. "Got prospects. Shipyard's hiring."

"Mr. Tucker mentioned it," Eliza said, trying to keep her voice level. "You should inquire tomorrow."

"Already did. I start Monday." He fumbled with his boot laces. "Now where's that eighteen pence? Man needs a drink after securing his family's future."

"It's for Harry's medicine," Eliza repeated firmly. "His cough's getting worse."

Thomas looked at his son as if noticing him for the first time. Harry had gone very still, watching the exchange with wide eyes.

"Coughing, are you, boy?" Thomas asked, his tone softening. "Coming down sick like your mother?"

The mention of Joy hung in the air between them. Harry shook his head quickly.

"Just a cold, Father. Nothing serious."

Thomas stared at him a moment longer, something like fear flickering across his face. Then he turned away, lying back on his pallet.

"Keep your coins," he muttered. "Buy the medicine. Boy needs his strength."

Relief flooded through Eliza. She helped her

father remove his boots, covering him with his thin blanket. Within minutes, Thomas began to snore.

Harry's voice came soft in the dimness. "Will we be all right, Liza?"

She looked at the loan agreement again, at the terms that could send them from poor to destitute in the space of a month. At Harry's thin face, so like their mother's. At their father, lost in the oblivion he sought more faithfully than anything else.

"Yes," she said with more conviction than she felt. "We'll find a way."

CHAPTER 2

Jonah Quinn set the crate down with a thud. Sweat ran down his back despite the chill that swept across the Thames. He straightened, pressing his palms against his lower back to ease the ache, and looked up at the sky. Evening approached as the sun hung low, barely visible through the mix of fog and coal smoke that perpetually shrouded the London docks.

"Quinn. Two more before you clock out."

Foreman Wallace pointed to a stack of crates still waiting to be unloaded from the Indian merchant vessel that had docked that morning. Wallace stood with his legs apart, his thumbs hooked in his belt, watching the men work with the detached interest of someone counting livestock.

"Yes, sir." Jonah wiped his hands on his trousers and moved toward the next crate.

Twelve hours of lifting, carrying, and stacking had turned his arms to lead. He welcomed the pain. Physical exhaustion meant sleep would come fast and without dreams. Five years of hiding from his past had taught him the value of dreamless nights.

The last two crates weighed more than the others, packed with something dense and unmarked. Probably contraband that would disappear before customs officials arrived tomorrow. Jonah knew better than to notice such things. Keeping his eyes down and his mouth shut had kept him alive since that night he'd plunged into the Thames, choosing the river's mercy over transportation to Australia.

"Put your back into it, Quinn." Wallace barked the order with casual cruelty.

Jonah gripped the edges of the crate and lifted with his legs, carrying it to join the others in the warehouse. The muscles in his forearms trembled. He'd grown stronger in his years as a dockworker, but nothing about the labor came naturally to him. His hands remembered the curves of wooden barrel staves, the precise tap of a cooper's hammer, not the rough heft of shipping crates.

The memory of his former trade swept through

him for an instant: the rich smell of oak, the satisfaction of bending wood to his will, Master Hargrove nodding with approval as Jonah completed a perfect seam. He pushed the thought away. That life belonged to a dead man.

"That's it for the day." Wallace marked something in his ledger. "Pay's on Friday."

The other men dispersed quickly, eager to reach pubs or homes or wherever they went to escape the endless labor of the docks. Jonah lingered, watching the water. The Thames flowed black and silent, carrying the waste of London out to sea. Sometimes he thought he could smell the rot beneath the surface, the accumulated filth of a city built on greed.

"You staying or going, Quinn?" Wallace fixed him with a suspicious stare.

"Going, sir." Jonah grabbed his coat. It was a secondhand wool garment with patched elbows and mismatched buttons.

He walked towards the dock exit. Not too fast, which might suggest guilt, nor too slow, which could draw unwanted attention. The right to exist in any space required a careful balance for a man who officially should not exist at all.

His boarding house stood four streets away, a

grim building packed with men like himself, laborers with no families, or none they acknowledged. Mrs. Pruitt, the owner, asked no questions beyond whether rent would be paid on time. The walls let through every sound from neighboring rooms: arguments, coughing, and the occasional sounds of purchased companionship.

Jonah turned away from the route that would take him there. Tonight, he couldn't bear the press of humanity, the smell of too many bodies confined in too little space. Instead, he headed toward the small tool shed at the edge of Blackwell Yard where he sometimes slept when solitude mattered more than comfort.

The yard keeper, Wilkes, had given him a key three months ago after finding Jonah asleep behind the crates one morning.

"Rather have you inside keeping the tools safe than outside where you might see things you shouldn't," Wilkes had said with the logic of a man who understood London's unwritten rules.

The arrangement cost Jonah a portion of his wages each week but bought him precious privacy when he needed it most.

He cut through a narrow passage between warehouses, his senses alert to the dangers that emerged after sunset. A group of men huddled around a fire in a metal barrel, passing a bottle between them. They watched him with dull eyes but made no move to stop him. Jonah kept his hand in his pocket, wrapped around the small knife he carried.

The fog got thicker as darkness fell and the gas lamps made weak circles of light that barely pushed back the gloom. Jonah knew the docks by feel as much as sight, finding his way by memory past the shadows of cranes and cargo.

He turned down the row where wool imports were stored before going to textile merchants. The space between the warehouses got narrower here, creating a tunnel of darkness even the fog couldn't fill. He slowed down, sensing something different in the familiar path.

Movement. Someone was moving through the shadows.

Jonah pressed himself against the rough brick wall, watching. Years of caution made him reach for his knife. Dockers knew better than to prowl the storage areas after hours. Anyone here now was after something that wasn't theirs.

The figure moved from shadow to shadow like they knew what they were doing. Small and slight, dressed in dark clothes, carrying what looked like an empty sack. A thief, then. Not unusual around the docks. Cargo disappeared daily despite the watchmen and their dogs.

After a few more steps, the figure passed through a patch of faint light from a distant lamp. Jonah caught a glimpse of a pale face, and hair tucked under a cap. Young. Female. This surprised him. Women rarely risked the docks at night unless they worked the taverns that served the sailors.

She moved toward the wool bales, checking over her shoulder as she went. Something about the way she moved seemed familiar, though Jonah couldn't place it. She wasn't a professional thief though, she was too cautious, and too obvious in her fear. A desperate amateur, then. More dangerous in some ways, because desperation made people unpredictable.

The sensible choice was to ignore her and continue to his shed. Her business wasn't his. Getting involved meant risk, and Jonah had survived by avoiding risks. He took a step to leave.

The girl reached the wool bales and ran her hand across one, testing the material. The gesture triggered a memory of his mother, checking fabric at the market, judging quality with the same quick touch. The connection made him stop.

He looked at her more carefully.

The girl pulled a small knife from her pocket and prepared to cut into one of the bales. Jonah knew the penalty for such theft. Transportation or worse, especially for someone with no connections to protect them.

He made his decision in a split second, against all the hard-learned caution of five years hiding in plain sight.

"You won't find good wool there," he called softly.

The girl froze. The knife disappeared into her pocket quick as lightning. She turned toward him, ready to run.

"Those bales are counted and weighed before distribution," Jonah continued, keeping his voice low. "Cut into one and they'll know. The penalty isn't worth the gain."

She didn't move, sizing him up. Jonah stayed where he was, with his hands where she could see them. The stance of someone who wasn't a threat.

"Who are you?" Her voice had no fear in it.

"Nobody important." Jonah took a small step forward. "But I know where the wool scraps get thrown away. Better quality than you'll find elsewhere, and no risk of the magistrate."

The girl didn't move, clearly trying to decide

whether to trust him or run. Jonah recognized the mental math of the desperate. Trust no one, but sometimes necessity forced cooperation.

"Why would you help me?" She kept her distance.

Fair question. One Jonah asked himself as the words left his mouth. He had no good answer except the truth.

"Because I know hunger when I see it." He pointed toward the far end of the warehouse row. "There's a waste bin behind the customs house. The inspectors cut samples from each shipment. They throw away the pieces after checking them. It's good quality wool, already cut into squares."

She studied him a moment longer. "And in exchange?"

The question surprised him. "Nothing."

This seemed to confuse her more than any threat might have. She shifted her weight from one leg to the other.

"Nobody gives something for nothing in London."

Jonah almost smiled at the bitter truth in her statement. "Consider it a favor to the Thames. One less body to fish out when you're caught cutting into cargo."

She took a half step toward him, moving into

better light. Her face showed youth but not innocence. Life had carved experience into her features that might have been pretty in different circumstances. Her clothes hung loose on her skinny frame but remained carefully mended.

"How do I reach this customs house?" she asked.

"Follow the warehouse line to the end. Turn left at the cooperage. The customs house stands across from the harbormaster's office." Jonah pointed the direction. "The waste bin sits against the east wall. Metal with a hinged lid. The night watchman makes rounds at the hour and half-hour, so plan accordingly."

She nodded once. "Thank you."

Jonah expected her to leave right away. Instead, she lingered, studying him until it made him uncomfortable. Few people looked at him anymore. He'd perfected the art of being invisible.

"You work the docks," she said. Not a question.

"Yes."

"You know the shipments. What comes in, what goes out."

Jonah tensed. This conversation had already gone on too long. "I load crates. That's all."

"But you notice things."

"Noticing things gets men killed." He stepped back into shadow. "Or transported."

Something in his tone made her expression change. The knowledge that came from surviving London's darker side.

"I'm Eliza Tate," she said suddenly, like the information was payment for his help.

The unexpected introduction caught Jonah off guard. Names meant connection. Connection meant danger. He should walk away without answering, keep up the isolation that kept him safe.

"Jonah Quinn," he heard himself say. "Dockworker. Former thief. Current nobody."

Her mouth turned up slightly. "At least you're honest."

"Sometimes honesty is all that can't be taken from you." The words came from some deep place he thought long buried.

The girl, Eliza, nodded like he'd confirmed something important. "Thank you."

With that, she slipped past him, moving quickly but no longer like she was hiding. Jonah watched her disappear into the fog. Only when he could no longer hear her did he continue toward his shed, wondering what madness had made him talk to her, offer help, and give his real name.

Five years of survival, and he'd risked it for a girl.

The tool shed stood where three storage buildings met, hidden in their shadow. Jonah unlocked the door and stepped into the small space. He lit the stub of candle he kept on the workbench, lighting up his refuge. An eight feet by six, with a roof that leaked when it rained and walls that let in the wind. Still, it offered solitude and safety, two things as valuable as gold in London.

He sat on the thin pallet he kept rolled in the corner, taking off his boots. They'd need fixing soon. The sole of the left one had worn thin, letting in water when he walked through puddles. Another expense he could barely afford.

From beneath the pallet, he pulled out a small box made of tin, once used for tobacco. Inside lay his savings of seven pounds, seven shillings, and sixpence. Not enough to start over somewhere new, but growing slowly toward that possibility.

He added his day's wages to the rest: four shillings for twelve hours of breaking his back. The coins clinked together, but at this rate, he'd need another three years before he could think about leaving London.

As he put the box back in its hiding place, his hand touched something else under the pallet. He paused, then pulled out the object he tried to forget he owned, a wooden cup, small enough to fit in his palm, carved with a pattern of oak leaves around the rim.

The last thing he'd made as an apprentice cooper. Master Hargrove had praised the work, declaring Jonah ready for journeyman status. A week later, Lockwood had accused him of theft, and everything had fallen apart.

Jonah ran his thumb over the carved leaves, feeling each ridge and curve. He remembered the pride he'd felt finishing it, the joy of turning raw wood into something useful and beautiful. No such feeling came from hauling crates twelve hours a day.

He set the cup aside and lay back on his pallet, staring at the shed's low ceiling. Sleep wouldn't come easy tonight, despite how tired his body felt. His mind kept going back to the moment when he'd spoken to her, the strange feeling of being seen after years of hiding.

"Fool," he muttered to himself. "Bloody fool."

Helping her had brought risk without reward. Speaking to her had broken his main rule of avoiding notice. Giving her his real name had been the act of a madman.

Yet as he closed his eyes, he found himself

wondering if she'd found the customs house, if she'd avoided the night watchman, if she'd found what she needed. The thoughts followed him into sleep, where for the first time in months, he dreamed not of drowning in the Thames but of a girl.

Morning came too quickly, and Jonah got up stiffly, his body complaining about yesterday's work. His throat felt raw, a warning of the cough that hit him each winter since his night in the river.

He splashed water on his face from the bucket he kept filled, the cold shock waking him fully. After pulling on his boots and coat, he left the shed, locking it behind him. The docks were already busy. Stevedores shouting to each other, cranes moving cargo, wagons arriving to collect yesterday's goods. The fog had pulled back some, showing the river's dull surface chopped by barges and tugboats.

Jonah took his usual route toward his work section, staying along the edge of the main yard to avoid talking to anyone. As he passed the customs house, he glanced toward the waste bin he'd told Eliza about. The lid was slightly open, suggesting someone had visited during the night.

Good. She'd found it. The thought made him feel oddly satisfied.

"Quinn! You're on the Miller shipment today."

Foreman Wallace waved him toward a newly docked ship where men already swarmed like ants around open cargo holds. Jonah raised a hand to show he heard and walked faster.

The Miller Line specialized in cloth imports from the northern manufacturing cities. Their ships carried wool and cotton for London's garment district. Heavy work, but clean compared to the coal ships or livestock transports.

"Take position three," Wallace ordered, checking names off his list. "We're short-handed today."

Jonah nodded and went to the assigned station. Position three meant working in the ship's hold directly, bringing cargo up to the dock rather than moving it to warehouses. Harder labor but better pay, five shillings instead of four for the day's work.

He went down the narrow stairs into the hold where bales of wool fabric filled the space in tight rows. The air smelled of the lanolin and chemicals used to treat the textiles. Two other men already worked there, creating a chain to pass bales up to the dock.

"Quinn's here," one called to the other. "Now we'll get moving."

Jonah recognized Patrick Byrne, an Irishman who'd worked the docks for decades. Beside him stood a younger man Jonah didn't know, with arms like tree trunks and a fresh scar across his chin.

"New man," Patrick explained, seeing Jonah's glance. "Tim Doyle. From Manchester."

Tim nodded hello but said nothing. Jonah returned the nod and took his position. They fell into the rhythm of work without talking. Words wasted energy better spent on lifting.

Hours passed in repetition. Lift, pass, return for the next. The hold gradually emptied as morning turned to afternoon. Jonah's muscles screamed, but he kept up the pace. Showing weakness meant being replaced. Being replaced meant no wages. No wages meant no food. The equation stayed simple no matter how complex the circumstances around it.

During a quick break to drink water from a shared bucket, Patrick came over beside him.

"Heard something you might want to know," the Irishman murmured, looking at the activity around them rather than at Jonah.

Jonah tensed. Patrick traded information and dock gossip to anyone who paid. That he offered something without being asked suggested trouble.

"What's that?" Jonah kept his voice neutral.

"The cargo inspector was asking about you this

morning. He wanted to know how long you've worked here, where you came from before."

The water turned to ash in Jonah's mouth. "What did Wallace tell him?"

"That you've been here four years, came from Liverpool docks. Nothing unusual."

Four years, not five. Liverpool, not nowhere. The small differences in Jonah's made-up history rarely mattered to men who paid little attention to their fellow workers beyond their ability to lift and carry.

"Who was asking?" Jonah put down the water dipper.

"I didn't catch a name. Well-dressed gent and not regular customs." Patrick scratched his grizzled chin. "Mentioned something about checking worker records against ship lists to look for patterns."

Patterns. The word sent ice through Jonah's veins. Pattern recognition meant someone had noticed something was off and maybe connected missing cargo to specific work crews. Such investigations usually ended with a few workers arrested. Innocent men chosen to keep authorities happy while the real thieves kept working.

Men with no connections. Men no one would miss. Men like Jonah Quinn, who had appeared from nowhere five years ago.

"Thanks for the warning." Jonah reached into his pocket and pressed a penny into Patrick's palm as payment for information that might save his freedom or his life.

Patrick pocketed the coin without looking at it. "Might be nothing. Might be something. Thought you should know."

The work started again with new urgency for Jonah. Each bale he lifted felt heavier than the last as his mind raced through options. If someone had taken special interest in him, he might need to disappear again. Change docks, perhaps. Change cities if necessary. The thought exhausted him almost as much as the lifting.

By late afternoon, the hold stood empty. Jonah climbed back to the dock, squinting in the fading daylight. His shirt stuck to his back with sweat despite the cold. His hands felt raw from the rough fabric of the wool bales.

Wallace approached with his ledger. "Good work today. Miller's paying bonus for finishing early. Extra shilling for each man."

Six shillings instead of five. A small fortune by Jonah's standards. Enough to consider meat for dinner instead of bread, or to add to his savings. The unexpected bonus should have cheered him up. Instead, it felt like payment for coming doom.

"Quinn." Wallace's voice stopped him as he turned to leave. "That customs man was asking about you. I told him you're one of my best workers."

Jonah managed a nod. "Appreciate that, sir."

"Don't make me a liar." Wallace gave him a hard stare. "Some of the night watchmen reported movement near the wool warehouses yesterday evening. Anything you want to tell me?"

Jonah kept eye contact despite wanting to look away.

"No, sir. I went straight to my lodgings after work."

Wallace studied him a moment longer, then made a mark in his ledger. "See that you continue to do so."

Jonah walked away, feeling like someone was watching him. Too many questions. Too much attention. The new life he'd maintained for five years had started to crack, and he couldn't tell how or why.

Rather than risk the main dock exit where officials might be waiting, Jonah took a roundabout route through the storage yards. He passed the customs house again, drawing his eyes to the waste bin where he'd sent Eliza. The lid was closed now, likely emptied during the day.

Had she found what she needed? Had she avoided getting caught? The questions bothered him more than they should. Her survival should mean nothing to him. His own hung by an increasingly thin thread.

Yet he found himself wondering if she would return. If helping her had been worth the risk. If the moment of connection, of being something other than invisible, justified the danger.

Lost in thought, he nearly bumped into a man turning the corner from the customs office. Jonah stepped back quickly, ducking his head in automatic deference.

"Pardon, sir."

"Mind your step," the man replied sharply, brushing past.

Jonah kept his gaze down, but not before catching a glimpse of a familiar face. His blood turned to ice in his veins, and it took all his control not to run or react. He forced himself to keep walking at a normal pace, fighting the urge to look back.

Augustus Lockwood. The merchant who had accused him of theft. The man whose testimony had sent him to transportation. The reason Jonah Quinn lived as a ghost in his own city.

Lockwood hadn't recognized him. Why would he? The young cooper's apprentice had died in the Thames five years ago according to official records. The bearded dockworker with rough hands and weathered skin shared little with that doomed young man.

Still, the meeting left Jonah shaking. He took a wrong turn in his rush to get away from Lockwood, ending up near the river's edge where cargo nets hung drying on wooden frames.

The Thames stretched before him, dark and uncaring. The same river that had nearly killed him now mocked him with how narrowly he'd escaped. Lockwood's presence at the docks couldn't be coincidence, not on the same day a customs inspector asked questions about Jonah's background.

He needed to disappear. Tonight. Take his savings and find another city, and another name.

The thought brought a tiredness that sank into his bones. He's always running. Always hiding. Always looking over his shoulder. Would he spend his whole life this way, never putting down roots, never making connections, never being more than a shadow?

As the last light faded from the sky, Jonah made his decision. He would return to his shed, collect his few things and savings, and be gone before dawn. Liverpool perhaps, or Bristol. Somewhere with docks and anonymous work, but far from Lockwood's reach.

The route back to his shed took him past the wool warehouses again. He moved quickly, wanting only to grab his things and vanish into London's vastness. The soft scuff of a boot against stone, followed by a muffled exclamation stopped him.

Jonah froze as someone moved in the shadows between warehouses. The same place he'd met Eliza the night before.

Against all logic and self-preservation, he turned toward the sound. A small figure darted between the crates, heading toward the spot where bales waited for tomorrow's distribution. Even in the poor light, he recognized her movements, and the set of her shoulders.

She had returned. After succeeding once, she had come back for more.

Jonah should walk away. His own situation had grown dangerous. He had no attention to spare for a ragpicker's problems, no matter how desperate. Helping her once had been risk enough. Doing so again, with Lockwood on the docks and questions being asked about him, was madness.

He took a step toward her anyway.

"Not there," he called softly. "The night watchman changed his route. Checks those bales every quarter hour now."

Eliza spun toward him, a knife already in her hand.

"You again." She lowered the knife but didn't put it away.

"Me again." Jonah glanced around, checking for witnesses to their conversation. "Did you find the customs bin?"

"Yes." She studied him in a way that seemed to cut through his blankness. "Good wool. Fetched four pence."

Four pence for risking arrest. The math of desperation. Jonah understood the calculation all too well.

"Not worth coming back for. They'll have changed the routine after finding the bin disturbed."

"I need more than four pence." Eliza's voice stayed firm. "My brother's medicine costs two shillings. Our rent just went up. My father…" She stopped.

Jonah recognized the half-sentence. Some burdens were too heavy to share with strangers. He should say goodnight and continue with his plan to leave London. Her troubles couldn't matter to him, not when his own survival hung in the balance.

"There's a better place," he heard himself say. "South dock. Shipment of mill ends came in yesterday. It off-cuts from the Manchester factories. Not prime quality, but better than scraps. They'll be loaded for distribution tomorrow morning."

Eliza's expression sharpened with interest. "Where exactly?"

"Warehouse Four. Back entrance faces the river. Lock's broken on the small door. Been that way for months because the night watchman uses it for smoke breaks." Jonah pointed southward. "Follow the river path. Count four buildings past the harbormaster's office. Wait until the clock strikes ten. Watchman Peters does his rounds then, leaves that section clear for half an hour."

She took in the directions carefully. "Why are you helping me?"

The question caught him off guard, though he'd asked himself the same thing. Why risk his safety for a girl he didn't know? Why offer information that could implicate him if she got caught?

"I don't know," he admitted.

His honesty seemed to surprise her as much as it surprised him. They stood in silence, two people balanced on the edge of London's unforgiving machinery, each recognizing in the other a shared knowledge of what survival cost.

"My brother has a cough that won't heal," Eliza said finally. "Our father drinks what he earns. We need three more shillings by week's end, or we lose our room."

Jonah nodded.

"I'm leaving London tomorrow," he said. "Someone's asking questions about me, so it's not safe anymore."

"Because you helped me?" Alarm crossed her face.

"No. Other reasons. Old troubles." Jonah looked toward the river, "Go to the South dock. Warehouse Four. Ten o'clock. You should find enough to fetch your three shillings."

She studied him a moment longer. "Will I see you again after tonight?"

The question carried no sentiment. Would her source of information disappear? Would this unlikely alliance end before it truly began?

"Not likely." Jonah felt an unexpected regret with the words. "Better that way."

Eliza nodded, accepting the reality without complaint. "Thank you. For tonight and yesterday."

"Good luck." He meant it more than she could know.

She turned to go, then paused. "Where will you go? After London."

"North maybe. Or west. Somewhere no one looks too hard at a man willing to work."

"I hope you find it." She spoke without false pity. "Somewhere they don't look too hard."

With that, she vanished into the gathering darkness. Jonah watched the space where she had stood, an unfamiliar feeling expanding in his chest. For five years, he had connected with no one, trusted no one, helped no one. Survival had consumed every thought and action.

Yet in the past two nights, he had chosen differently. Had remembered, however briefly, what it felt like to be more than a ghost drifting through London's underworld. The feeling disoriented him, like a limb waking up after too long without blood.

He turned away, continuing toward his shed. His plan hadn't changed. He'd collect his things and savings, then vanish before dawn. London had become too dangerous to stay.

Yet as he walked, Jonah found himself thinking of different routes. If he left after midnight instead of at dawn, he might pass Warehouse Four on his way.

He might see if Eliza found what she sought, and he could make sure she left safely before he disappeared from London forever.

A pointless risk. A stupid delay. He would make the detour anyway.

The realization didn't shock him as much as it should have. Something had shifted these past two nights, some frozen part of himself was beginning to thaw. Whatever danger London now held for him, he would face it for a few hours longer, if only to know that his final act in this city that had both saved and condemned him had made some small difference.

Jonah Quinn, supposed thief, presumed drowned, would help a ragpicker girl find wool scraps worth three shillings. Then he would disappear again, taking with him the strange comfort that for one brief moment, someone had seen him as he truly was, and had looked back without judgment.

CHAPTER 3

*S*ix pence. That's what Rosie paid for the cotton scraps. Not much, but enough to shut up Mr. Finch for a bit. Eliza counted the coins twice before handing them over, watching Finch's face for any hint of pity.

"That leaves three shillings still due," Finch said, pocketing the money without writing anything down. His fingers were all stained with ink.

"I know." Eliza stood up straight. No begging. Never that. "I need another week for the rest."

Finch scratched his beard and did some math in his head. He wasn't the worst landlord in Spitalfields. He didn't seem to enjoy tossing folks out. Just wanted his money.

"One week," he agreed. "Not a day more. The

council's breathing down my neck about these rent increases."

"Thank you." Eliza turned to leave.

"The boy still coughing?" Finch called after her.

She stopped, surprised he'd asked. "Yes."

"Mrs. Finch says to try onions in sugar water. It worked for our youngest last winter."

Well, that was unexpected. Eliza nodded and hurried downstairs, not wanting him to see how close to breaking she felt.

Outside, the rain soaked through her shawl in minutes. November in London was miserable. Cold, wet, and gray. A week to find three more shillings. No way she'd manage that with regular ragpicking, especially with Harry too sick to help. The wool from the docks had saved them once. She needed more.

At home, Harry sat by their tiny fire, wrapping rags around his feet to keep warm.

"Did Mr. Finch take the money?" he asked, his voice scratchy from all the coughing.

"Yes. We have another week." Eliza hung her wet shawl by the fire. "Any sign of Father?"

Harry shook his head. Thomas Tate had stormed out three days ago after they'd fought about the Lockwood loan. Usually, he'd come back drunk and sorry after a day or two, but this time felt different. He'd looked scared before he left.

"I made soup," Harry said, pointing to a pot of watery broth with potato peelings floating in it. "Found the vegetables behind the market."

"Clever boy." Eliza ruffled his hair. No point mentioning that those "vegetables" were just scraps nobody else wanted. "Smells good."

They ate without talking much, saving half for their father just in case. After dinner, Harry fell asleep fast. Poor kid was worn out from all that coughing. Eliza sat by the fire, fixing a hole in her only other skirt and trying to figure out what to do.

Three shillings in a week. Rosie might front her a few pennies for mending work, but nowhere near enough. The docks were her best chance, if she could find good wool scraps again.

If she could find Jonah Quinn again.

Thinking about the dockworker made her feel all mixed up. Grateful he'd helped. Suspicious about why. Curious about why a man who clearly wanted to stay invisible would risk helping her. His last words stuck in her head: "I'm leaving London tomorrow." Had he gone already? For some reason, that thought bothered her.

Sleep came in fits and starts, broken up by

Harry's coughing and the big question of what she'd do if Jonah had disappeared. By morning, she'd made up her mind: she had to find him first.

"I need to go out," she told Harry after breakfast of crust of bread split between them. "Will you be all right alone?"

"I'm not a baby." Harry wrapped his blanket tighter. "Where are you going?"

"Back to the docks. The wool scraps brought good money. We need more."

Harry looked at her face, reading her like he always could. "Be careful. The constables patrol there."

"I will." She tucked the blanket around him better. "Try Mr. Finch's remedy. Onion water with sugar. For your cough."

Harry made a face but nodded. Eliza checked their tiny pile of coal, making sure he had enough to keep the fire going, then headed out into the cold morning.

The walk to the docks took forever. Eliza used the time to practice what she'd say when she found Jonah Quinn. If she found him. The man had his own troubles, that much was obvious from their quick meetings. He owed her nothing. Expected nothing. But something in his eyes when he'd helped her suggested there was more to him than just a man doing a good deed.

The docks were huge and busy, even in the nasty weather. Men were carrying crates and barrels everywhere. Bosses shouted orders. Clerks checked lists. Finding one guy in all this mess seemed impossible.

Eliza walked up to some dockworkers eating lunch under an awning. The men looked at her curiously but not mean.

"Excuse me," she said. "I'm looking for someone who works here. Jonah Quinn."

The men exchanged looks. One shook his head. Another just kept eating. Only the oldest guy, with white hair and skin like old leather, answered.

"Quinn? Works over in Blackwell section, loading cloth shipments mostly." He pointed east. "Keeps to himself, that one. What's your business?"

"Family matter," Eliza lied easy as breathing. "His mother sent me."

The old man laughed. "Tell his mother she raised a quiet one. Five years loading ships and the man hasn't said fifty words total."

Five years? Not leaving London yesterday, then. Another lie, or he changed plans?

"Where would I find him now?" she asked.

"Try Warehouse Six. Miller shipment came in this morning. Quinn's crew is handling it."

Eliza thanked him and walked toward the big buildings at the dock's east end. The rain was coming down harder, driving most workers under cover. She pulled her shawl over her head, knowing she stuck out like a sore thumb, being a woman in this man's world.

Warehouse Six loomed ahead, doors wide open showing men moving cargo inside. Eliza paused at the entrance, searching for Jonah's big shoulders and careful way of moving.

"You can't be here." A boss with a ledger blocked her way. "Dock rules. No strangers allowed."

"I need to speak with Jonah Quinn," Eliza said, standing firm. "Family emergency."

The boss squinted at her. "Quinn? No visitors during work hours. He finishes at six. Wait outside the gates like everyone else."

"Please. It's urgent."

"It's always urgent." The boss pointed toward the main gate. "Six o'clock. Not a minute sooner."

There was no point arguing, it would just draw attention. Eliza nodded and walked away, but instead of leaving, she found a spot between some crates where she could watch the warehouse without being seen. The rain soaked through everything she wore, making her shiver. Six hours to wait, if the boss had told the truth. Six hours in freezing rain.

Worth it if it meant keeping their room. Worth it for Harry.

Time crawled by. Workers came and went, but no Jonah. Eliza stamped her feet to keep her blood moving, cursing the November cold that went straight to her bones. By late afternoon, her teeth were chattering and she couldn't feel her fingers anymore.

"You'll catch your death waiting in this weather."

The voice came from behind. Eliza spun around to find Jonah Quinn standing a few feet away, carrying a crate on one shoulder like it was nothing.

"You're still here," she blurted out.

"Looks that way." He set the crate down, glancing around to make sure nobody saw them talking. "Why are you?"

"I need your help." It hurt her pride to admit it, but she was desperate. "The cotton scraps bought us a week before we're tossed out, that's all. We need three shillings by Sunday or we lose our room."

Jonah's face gave nothing away. "So you came looking for more free information."

"Not free." Eliza pulled two pennies from her pocket, half of what they had left. "I can pay."

He looked at the coins, then at her face. Something changed in his expression.

"Put that away," he said quietly. "I don't need your pennies."

"I don't take charity."

"Neither do I. But I don't take a child's bread money either."

They stared at each other, stuck at a standoff. Eliza shivered again, couldn't help it after hours in the rain.

"You're soaked through," Jonah said. "Wait here."

He disappeared into the warehouse before she could answer. Eliza almost left - her pride telling her to go, common sense telling her to stay. Common sense won. Pride never filled empty bellies.

A few minutes later, Jonah came back with a burlap sack. "Put this around your shoulders. Not pretty, but dry."

Eliza hesitated, then took it. The rough sack smelled like coffee beans, but it kept the rain off.

"Thank you." She wrapped it around her shoulders. "Does this mean you'll help us?"

"It means I don't want your death from pneumonia on my conscience." Jonah checked the sky, then moved her deeper into the shelter of the crates. "I have an hour left on shift. Say what you came to say."

"I told you. We need money for rent. The wool scraps helped once. I need to know where to find more."

"And I told you I'm leaving London." His face darkened. "Plans changed, but the danger hasn't. Someone's asking questions about me and being seen with you doubles that risk."

"Yet here you stand," Eliza pointed out. "Talking to me anyway."

That hung in the air between them. Jonah looked away first.

"What do you want from me?" he asked.

"Information. You know which ships bring wool. Which warehouses throw away good scraps. Tell me, and I'll do the rest."

"It's not that simple. Dock security's tighter after some recent thefts. More watchmen, more patrols." Jonah lowered his voice. "They think someone inside is helping thieves. That's why they're checking on workers' backgrounds."

"Then we need a different deal." Eliza thought fast. "You can't risk being seen helping me take things from the docks. But what if I bring you something instead?"

His eyebrow went up a bit. "What could you possibly bring me?"

"Food." The one thing they had that might be worth something. "Real food, not the slop they sell at dock canteens. Three times a week I'll bring you a hot meal. In exchange, you tell me which ships bring valuable cargo, when they unload, where they throw out the good scraps."

"You can barely feed yourself and your brother."

"I manage." Eliza lifted her chin. "Do we have a deal?"

Jonah studied her face like he was trying to figure something out. His stare made her want to look away, but she didn't.

"Two conditions," he said finally. "First, you never tell anyone about our arrangement. Second, you bring food only to my shed, after dark, not to the docks where people might see us together."

"Your shed?"

"Where I sleep sometimes. It's safer than my boarding house when I need privacy."

The fact that he'd trust her with where he slept didn't escape Eliza. Trust was hard to come by in London.

"Agreed." She held out her hand to make it official.

Jonah hesitated before taking it. His palm felt rough against hers, hardened by years of work. They only touched for a second, but it left a warmth that spread up her arm.

"East dock," he said, letting go of her hand. "A merchant ship Valiant arrives Thursday. Scottish wool for Kensington tailors. Good stuff with plenty of leftover bits. Inspection happens Friday morning. Scraps go to the waste heap behind Warehouse Four by noon. Watch for the customs men, they check papers between shipments."

Eliza memorized every word. "Thursday arrival. Friday disposal. Warehouse Four."

"The shed is at the south end of Blackwell Yard. It's a small building by itself, next to the cooperage. Come Monday after dark. I'll leave the padlock open."

"I'll be there." Eliza handed back the burlap sack. "Thank you."

Jonah took it, his face impossible to read. "Don't thank me yet. This arrangement brings risk to us both."

"Risk is nothing new." She pulled her damp shawl tighter. "Not in Spitalfields."

"No. I suppose not." He glanced toward the warehouse. "I need to finish my shift. Go home, get dry. Your brother needs you alive."

The mention of Harry reminded Eliza how much time had passed. "Yes. Of course."

She turned to leave, then stopped. "Why did you lie about leaving London?"

Jonah went very still. "Why did you lie about offering to pay for information when you need those pennies for food?"

The question caught her off guard. She could deny it, but what was the point? They both knew what it took to survive.

"Pride," she admitted. "And you?"

"Caution." His eyes met hers. "We all protect what matters, Eliza Tate."

Hearing him say her name gave her an odd feeling in her chest, like being recognized as a real person in a city that saw most people as just problems.

"Monday after dark," she confirmed. "I'll bring stew."

For just a second, something like a smile touched his mouth. "Until then."

Eliza left the docks feeling lighter somehow, despite her wet clothes and cold bones. She'd found him. Made a deal. Found a way to get the money they needed. The cost, three meals a week they could barely afford seemed worth it compared to losing their room.

The walk home took her through streets getting busy as evening came on. Workers headed home from factories, sellers shouted about the last of their goods, and the pubs filled with people wanting warmth and drink. Eliza avoided Brick Lane, taking quieter streets where constables didn't bother patrolling.

As she passed an alley near Whitechapel Road, she heard shouting. A boy about twelve years old ran out of the narrow passage with a constable chasing him. The kid clutched a small basket of apples, obviously stolen from a nearby stall.

"Stop! Thief!" The constable blew his whistle. "Stop in the name of the law!"

The boy ran straight toward Eliza, terror all over his face. Behind him, the constable was catching up with his club already out. Eliza recognized him. He was Burke, known for breaking the fingers of children he caught stealing instead of bothering to arrest them.

Making a split-second decision, Eliza stepped forward just as the boy passed, deliberately tripping him. They both fell to the ground, and the apples spilled across the muddy street. She grabbed the boy's arm like she was catching him.

"You little wretch!" she yelled for the constable to hear. "Watch where you're running!"

Burke arrived, breathing hard. "Stand aside, girl. That boy's a thief."

Eliza kept hold of the struggling child. "This boy? He knocked me over running from someone, but he's no thief. He's my brother Tommy, simple in the head. Mother sent us for bread."

"He stole apples from Cowell's stand," Burke insisted. "Saw him with my own eyes."

"Apples?" Eliza looked at the fruit scattered on the ground. "We can't afford apples. Must be someone else you're after. This is Tommy. Tell the nice constable your name, Tommy."

The boy stared at her, confused but hopeful.

"T-Tommy," he stammered. "Sorry for running, sister."

Burke squinted suspiciously. "He looks nothing like you."

"Different fathers," Eliza said without missing a beat. "Mine was Irish. His was from up north."

The explanation made Burke pause. Around here, nobody asked too many questions about who fathered who. He looked at the apples, then down the street where the real thief might have escaped while he was delayed.

"If I find out you're lying," he threatened, "I'll remember your face."

"As I'll remember yours," Eliza replied, just humble enough to avoid being called disrespectful. "God bless your work keeping us safe, Constable."

The sweet talk worked. Burke stood taller, pleased to be important.

"Keep better watch on your simple brother," he said. "Streets aren't safe after dark."

"Yes, sir. Thank you, sir." Eliza pulled the boy's arm. "Come along, Tommy. Mother's waiting."

They walked away quickly but didn't run, which would look guilty. Only when they turned onto a quieter street did Eliza let go of the boy's arm.

"You're safe now," she said. "He's gone."

The boy stared at her with big eyes. "Why'd you help me?"

"Burke breaks thieves' fingers. Bit much for a few apples."

"They weren't for eating," the boy admitted. "For selling. Three for a penny down Petticoat Lane."

Eliza nodded, understanding completely. "What's your real name? Not Tommy, I'm guessing."

"Ben. Some call me Penny-Ben 'cause I can make a penny stretch further than anyone." Pride filled his voice despite his ragged clothes. "You're the ragpicker girl. From Fern Street."

That surprised her. "How do you know where I live?"

"I know lots of things." Ben tapped his forehead. "Information's valuable. Like knowing which constables take bribes and which break bones. Or which ragpickers help strangers for no reason."

His sharp assessment reminded Eliza that street children survived by being clever, not innocent. This one had the sharp eyes of a boy who noticed everything and the quick mouth of someone who traded in secrets.

"Information is valuable," she agreed. "Do you trade fairly?"

Ben thought about this. "Depends what you want to know."

"I need to learn about a man named Lockwood. Augustus Lockwood. He runs workhouses on the east side."

The name changed Ben's face completely. Fear replaced his confidence, and he stepped back.

"I don't talk about Lockwood," he said, whispering now. "Bad business, that. Very bad."

"My father owes him money," Eliza explained. "I need to know what happens when people can't pay."

Ben looked around like he thought Lockwood might jump out of the shadows.

"They say he owns half the workhouses now," he said quietly. "But that's not where the money comes from. It's the children. He sends them north to the factories. Calls it apprenticeships, but nobody ever comes back."

Eliza felt cold in a way that had nothing to do with her wet clothes. "He sells children?"

"Not sells. Rents." Ben's eyes darted around nervously. "Look, I've said too much. Ask someone else about Lockwood. I want no part of it."

"Wait." Eliza pulled one of her precious pennies from her pocket. "For the information. And for not telling anyone we talked."

Ben took the coin, looking surprised. "You're paying me? After I stole them apples?"

"Information has value. You said so yourself."

The boy pocketed the penny quick as lightning. "What else do you want to know?"

"Nothing now. But I might need your eyes and ears again sometime." Eliza looked at his skinny face. "Do you have a place to sleep tonight?"

"I manage." The words echoed what she'd told

Jonah earlier. "Church steps if it rains too hard. Doorways if it don't."

"If you need warmth, the baker on Bell Lane leaves his ovens cooling overnight. Back door's never locked right."

Ben nodded, storing the tip away. "I'll remember that. And I'll remember you helped me." He turned to go, then looked back. "They call me Penny-Ben, but my real name's Benjamin Wilkes. If you need information, ask for me at the Bull and Crown. Potboy there's my cousin."

"Eliza Tate," she offered in return. "Fern Street, like you already knew."

Ben grinned. "Might be I notice things now and then. Might be I'll notice if Lockwood's men come sniffing around your building." He touched his cap in a surprise show of manners. "Good evening, Miss Tate."

He vanished into the darkness with the easy grace of a kid who stayed alive by not being seen. Eliza kept walking home, and by the time she reached Fern Street, night had fallen completely. She climbed the stairs to their room, eager to see Harry despite how tired and hungry she felt. The door was partly open, lantern light spilling into the hallway.

"Harry?" she called, pushing it open.

What she saw stopped her cold. Harry sat on his pallet, eyes wide with fear. Beside him, their father lay unconscious, face beaten so badly she barely recognized him, a d he had blood in his hair. And standing over them both was a man she'd never seen before, smiling to show a gold tooth that caught the lantern light.

"Miss Tate, I presume." The man's voice sounded fancy despite his rough looks. "Silas Grady, representing Mr. Lockwood. Your father and I have business to discuss when he wakes. About his debt. Which has, unfortunately, gone up a bit due to interest."

Eliza stepped into the room, putting herself between Grady and Harry.

"What have you done to him?" she demanded.

"Just encouraged prompt payment. Mr. Lockwood doesn't like waiting for what he's owed." Grady pulled a paper from his coat. "The new total comes to six shillings, due by month's end. Plus one shilling penalty for late payment this week."

"Seven shillings?" Eliza couldn't hide her shock. "That's robbery."

"That's business." Grady's smile never reached his eyes. "Mr. Lockwood understands your situation is... difficult. He offers an alternative."

"What alternative?"

"The boy could work off part of the debt. Healthy children are always needed in the workhouses. After a year or two of service, we'd consider it settled."

Harry made a frightened noise behind her. Eliza reached back to squeeze his hand without taking her eyes off Grady.

"My brother stays with me," she said firmly. "We'll pay the seven shillings."

"Seven by month's end," Grady confirmed. "In full. No partial payments." He stepped toward the door. "Do give your father my regards when he wakes. Remind him that next time, breaking bones costs extra."

After he left, Eliza locked the door and dragged their only chair against it just to be safe. Harry threw himself into her arms, crying into her still-damp dress.

"I thought he would take me," the boy sobbed. "He said the workhouse needed strong boys."

"No one's taking you anywhere." Eliza held him tight, trying to figure out how they'd ever get seven shillings. "I promise. We'll find a way."

Harry pulled back, wiping his eyes. "Father came home just before that man got here. He was already hurt. Said he tried to win money at cards to pay our debt, but lost instead. Then that man knocked him down and said it was a warning."

Eliza looked at Thomas Tate's beaten face. Blood dried around his nose and mouth, one eye swollen shut. How could he pay anything now? He couldn't work like this, and seven shillings might as well be seven pounds for all they could manage to scrape together.

"Help me get him onto his pallet," she said to Harry.

Together they moved Thomas, who moaned but didn't wake up. Eliza cleaned his wounds with water from their bucket, noting the split lip, the cut above his eye that would leave another scar. When she'd done what she could, she covered him with their only blanket.

"Will he die?" Harry whispered.

"No." Eliza sounded more sure than she felt. "He's tough, our father. Survived worse than this."

They ate the rest of Harry's potato soup without talking, both too tired for words. Harry fell asleep curled against her side, warm despite how cold the room was. Eliza stayed awake long after, staring at the ceiling and rethinking her plans.

Seven shillings. Impossible through ragpicking alone.

Impossible even with Jonah's information about wool shipments.

The shed. Monday after dark. She'd still go, but now she needed more than information. She needed a miracle, or at least a plan that would bring in seven shillings in the next two weeks.

CHAPTER 4

Jonah hauled another sack of grain onto his shoulder, his muscles burning in silent protest. The weight itself was nothing, he'd carried heavier, but this marked the forty-third sack in two hours. The constant bending, lifting, and carrying had transformed his body into one unified ache.

"Quinn! Put your back into it!" bellowed Foreman Wallace from his perch near the gangplank. The man never lifted anything heavier than a cup of ale these days, but he had a remarkable ability to spot any worker who paused for even a second.

"Yes, sir," Jonah muttered, quickening his pace across the wooden planks.

The morning had dawned gray and damp, typical

London weather that seemed determined to match his mood. Fog clung to the Thames like a mourner's shroud, obscuring the far shore and muffling the constant cacophony of the docks. Gulls swooped overhead, their harsh cries cutting through the rhythmic grunts and curses of the dockworkers.

Jonah deposited the sack in the growing pile inside the warehouse and wiped sweat from his brow with a forearm. Five years of this work had hardened his body, turned his hands to leather, but it never got easier. Not really. The work simply became a familiar misery.

"Oi, Quinn!" called Roy, a barrel-chested man with a perpetually ruddy face. "You hear the news?"

Jonah shook his head, already moving back toward the ship for another load. Roy fell into step beside him.

"His Lordship's gracing us with his presence today." Roy's voice dripped with sarcasm. "Augustus bloody Lockwood himself, coming to inspect his latest shipment."

The name stopped Jonah mid-stride. "Lockwood? Here? Today?"

"That's what I hear. McManus over at the customs house says they're rolling out the red carpet." Roy spat on the ground. "Figure the bastard wants to make sure none of us poor souls are pinching his precious cargo."

Jonah's mind raced. He'd glimpsed Lockwood just the other day, but the man hadn't seen him, hadn't recognized the cooper's apprentice he'd destroyed five years ago in the face of the weathered dockworker Jonah had become. But a closer encounter? That was a risk he couldn't afford.

"When?" Jonah asked, his voice carefully controlled.

"Afternoon, they say. Big important man like that doesn't rise with the working folk, does he?" Roy chuckled, oblivious to Jonah's tension. "Better look busy, though. They'll be watching extra close today."

Jonah nodded and forced himself back to work, though his thoughts were suddenly far from the grain sacks. He'd planned to leave London anyway, this just accelerated things. He could collect his pay at midday, gather his meager possessions, and be on his way before Lockwood arrived.

But then Eliza Tate's face flashed in his mind. He'd promised her information about valuable cargo, a way to make more than the pittance she earned picking scraps. If he disappeared now...

He cursed under his breath. Why should he care? She was just another desperate East End soul, no different from the hundreds he encountered daily. Her problems weren't his.

Yet he couldn't quite convince himself of that.

Jonah worked through the morning, and by midday, the ship's hold was nearly empty, and Foreman Wallace called the break. The men shuffled toward the makeshift canteen area, a collection of crates and barrels where they could sit and eat whatever food they'd brought.

Jonah had just settled on an upturned barrel, unwrapping the hunk of bread he'd purchased earlier, when a commotion at the dock entrance caught his attention. Two well-dressed men strode toward the customs office, surrounded by a small entourage. Even from this distance, Jonah recognized the taller figure's imperious bearing.

"That's them already?" he muttered.

"Seems His Majesty couldn't wait," observed Roy, dropping down beside him. "And look who's with him, Silas bloody Grady."

Jonah's eyes shifted to the second figure. Shorter than Lockwood but moving with a predatory grace that sent a chill down his spine. Silas Grady—Lockwood's enforcer and debt collector. The man whose job it was to know faces, to hunt down those who attempted to cheat his employer.

Unlike Lockwood, who might not immediately recognize the boy he'd wronged in the man Jonah had become, Grady was a different threat entirely. The man made it his business to remember faces.

"I need to go," Jonah said abruptly, wrapping his bread back in its cloth.

Roy raised an eyebrow. "Break's hardly started. Where you off to?"

"Got something to take care of," Jonah replied vaguely, already standing. "Cover for me with Wallace if he asks?"

Without waiting for an answer, Jonah turned and walked casually toward the back of the warehouse. Once out of sight of the other workers, he quickened his pace, weaving between stacks of crates toward the side exit. He needed to be gone before—

"You there! Dockhand!"

Jonah froze at the sharp voice behind him. Slowly, he turned, keeping his head slightly bowed, cap pulled low over his eyes.

Silas Grady stood fifteen feet away, one hand resting casually on the walking stick he carried, a walking stick Jonah knew concealed a thin, sharp blade. The years had added a few lines around Grady's eyes, but otherwise he looked much the same with his expensive coat, polished boots, and that perpetual smirk that suggested he found the world's suffering amusing.

"Yes, sir?" Jonah pitched his voice lower than normal, rougher.

Grady approached, his head tilted slightly as he studied Jonah. "You're not supposed to be back here during inspection. All workers should be in the designated break area."

"Sorry, sir. Just needed to fetch something I forgot."

Grady came closer still, his eyes narrowing. "Have we met before? Your face seems familiar."

Jonah's pulse thundered in his ears. "Don't think so, sir. Been working the docks five years now."

"Five years..." Grady mused, still staring at him with uncomfortable intensity. "What's your name?"

"Quinn, sir. Jonah Quinn."

Something flickered across Grady's face, skepticism, perhaps, or the first glimmer of recognition. Just as Jonah was calculating whether he could make it to the door before Grady could raise an alarm, a voice called from the front of the warehouse.

"Grady! Mr. Lockwood needs you. Customs paperwork issue."

Grady hesitated, visibly annoyed at the interruption. He pointed his walking stick at Jonah. "Stay right there, Quinn. I want to finish our chat."

He turned and walked briskly toward the front of the warehouse. The moment he was out of sight, Jonah bolted for the side door. Once outside, he ducked into the narrow alley between warehouses, moving quickly but not running because running would attract attention.

His mind raced as fast as his feet. Grady had recognized something in him, maybe not the full truth, but enough to make him suspicious. And a suspicious Silas Grady was as dangerous as a rabid dog. If he mentioned his concerns to Lockwood, if they started asking questions...

Jonah needed to collect his pay and disappear. Now. Today. His room at the boarding house contained little worth taking, some clothes, a spare pair of boots, a small knife, and the money he'd managed to save. He could be at the coaching inn by early evening, on a wagon heading north by nightfall.

But as he navigated through the warren of alleys that flanked the docks, another thought nagged at him. Eliza Tate. The debt her father owed to Lockwood. The threat to her brother.

"Not your problem," he muttered to himself as he

emerged onto a wider street, blending into the flow of people. "She's not your responsibility."

Even as he said it, though, he knew it wasn't that simple. He slowed his pace. He wasn't going to leave just yet. He couldn't.

* * *

Jonah spent the rest of the afternoon in a dim pub two streets away from the docks, nursing a single ale while watching the door. Every time it opened, his muscles tensed, ready to flee if Grady's lean figure appeared in the doorway. The crowded establishment offered some anonymity, but he'd chosen a corner table with a clear path to the back exit, just in case.

His fingers drummed against the scarred wooden tabletop as he weighed his options. The dockmaster owed him three days' wages, but returning to collect it would be madness now that Grady's suspicions were aroused. Better to write it off as a loss. His meager savings would have to suffice until he could find work elsewhere.

As the afternoon shadows lengthened outside the grimy windows, he realized he needed to return to the shed, and soon. Eliza would be expecting to meet him at the shed behind Warehouse Four. Their arrangement had seemed simple enough yesterday. Now it seemed like a terrible complication.

Abandoning his half-finished ale, Jonah slipped out the back door of the pub and took a circuitous route toward the docks, sticking to side streets and staying alert for any sign of pursuit. The first stars were appearing in the darkening sky by the time he reached the weathered shed that had become their meeting place.

He leaned against the rough wooden wall, pulling his coat tighter against the evening chill. The sensible thing would be to leave immediately, collect his things and vanish into the night. Yet here he stood, waiting for a wisp of a girl with fierce blue eyes and a brother to protect.

"Fool," he muttered to himself.

The soft scuff of footsteps made him straighten. Jonah melted deeper into the shadows, watching as a slight figure approached the shed, carrying something wrapped in cloth. Even in the dim light, he recognized Eliza's determined stride.

"You're actually here," she said as she spotted him, relief evident in her voice. "I wasn't sure you would be."

"I said I would be," he replied, stepping forward.

"Men say a lot of things." She handed him the bundle. "It's not much, just bread and cheese and a bit of cold meat pie. Probably not what you're used to."

Jonah unwrapped the cloth to find the promised meal, still warm from being carried against her body. It was simple food, but fresh and undoubtedly prepared with care. His stomach growled in response.

"It's more than enough," he said honestly, rewrapping it. "Thank you."

"Well?" Eliza crossed her arms, her expression expectant. "Your turn. What can you tell me about valuable cargo? Where should I look? When's the best time?"

Jonah studied her face in the growing darkness and the determined set of her chin, the hope in her eyes that she was trying to hide behind practicality. The weight of what he was about to do settled in his chest.

"I'm sorry, Eliza. I can't go through with our arrangement."

Her face hardened immediately. "What? But I brought you food...we had a deal!"

"I know," he said, holding up a hand. "And I'm not trying to cheat you." He reached into his pocket and pulled out several coins, holding them out to her. "Here. This will cover your brother's medicine for at least a month. Take it."

Eliza stared at the offered money, suspicion replacing anger. "Why would you give me that? What's the catch?"

"No catch. I just..." He struggled to find the right words. "Lockwood had men at the docks today. They're increasing security. It's not safe for you to be poking around the warehouses."

"I can handle myself," she insisted, though her eyes kept darting to the coins in his hand.

"Not against men like Lockwood and his enforcers," Jonah said, his voice dropping. "You don't understand how dangerous they are. How far they'll go."

Something in his tone must have reached her because her defiance wavered. "I don't accept charity."

"It's not charity. Consider it payment for the meal." He took her hand and pressed the coins into her palm, closing her fingers around them. "And for your silence about our meetings here."

Eliza looked down at the money in her hand, then back up at him. "This is more than a few meals' worth."

"Then I'm overpaying. So be it."

She shook her head slowly. "You're strange, Jonah Quinn." She pocketed the money nonetheless. "But I won't pretend this doesn't help."

Relief flooded through him, but he knew this money alone wouldn't solve her problems.

"Listen," he said, "I know someone at St. Anne's churchyard. Martha Hughes. She takes in mending work, clothes, linens, that sort of thing."

"Mending?" Eliza's eyebrows rose. "I know how to sew."

"She's always complaining she has more work than hands. Pays fair wages too. Tell her I sent you."

"You know a seamstress?" Skepticism colored her voice. "How?"

"She mended my coat last winter," he said, which was true enough, though he omitted that Martha had also tended the knife wound in his side when he couldn't risk a proper doctor. "She's a good woman. Respectable work."

Eliza's fingers touched the coins in her pocket, as if reassuring herself they were real. "Why are you helping me?"

The simple question caught him off guard. Why was he helping her? He'd spent years avoiding attachments of any kind. So why was he helping her.

"Maybe I don't like seeing Lockwood destroy more lives," he finally answered. "Take the money. Go to Martha. And Eliza..." His voice grew serious. "Don't cross Lockwood. Whatever your father owes him, it isn't worth what that man will do to collect."

A shadow crossed her face. "He's threatened to take Harry to the workhouse if we don't pay."

The familiar surge of hatred toward Lockwood burned in Jonah's chest. "All the more reason to stay away from his warehouses. You get caught stealing, and you won't be able to help your brother at all."

Eliza stood silent for a long moment, then nodded. "Thank you," she said quietly. "For the money. And the advice about Martha."

"You're welcome." He gestured with his chin toward the main road. "Go on now. It's not safe for you to be out after dark."

She hesitated, looking like she wanted to say something else, then simply nodded again and turned to leave. Jonah watched her disappear into the shadows, her slender figure soon swallowed by the darkness.

When he was certain she was gone, he sagged against the wall of the shed, running a hand over his face. He should be miles away by now. Grady had almost recognized him. Lockwood was taking a personal interest in the docks. Every instinct honed by five years of hiding screamed at him to flee.

Instead, he was making plans to stay. Making connections. Putting himself at risk for a girl he barely knew.

"You damned fool," he muttered to himself, thumping his head lightly against the wooden wall. "Throwing away caution to the wind for a pair of blue eyes and a sad story."

CHAPTER 5

*E*liza hurried home through the darkening streets, clutching the small paper package of medicine against her chest like it contained diamonds instead of powders that smelled like chalk and tasted worse. The apothecary had charged her four pence for it - highway robbery, really - but she'd paid without complaint. Harry needed it.

Jonah Quinn's coins still felt strange in her pocket. She'd spent only what was necessary for Harry's medicine, and she would the rest hidden in her special spot at home. It wasn't charity, she reminded herself.

As she approached their building, she quickened her pace. The sooner she got this medicine into Harry, the sooner his fever might break. She took the stairs two at a time, ignoring the protest in her tired legs.

"Harry, I'm back," she called, pushing open their door. "I've got your medicine—"

The words died in her throat. Harry sat huddled on his thin mattress, knees pulled to his chest, face streaked with tears. His shoulders shook with each sob.

Eliza dropped to her knees beside him. "What is it? Has your fever gotten worse?" She pressed her palm to his forehead. Hot, but no hotter than before.

Harry shook his head, unable to speak through his tears. Instead, he pointed toward the loose floorboard in the corner.

"What?" Eliza's stomach dropped. "Harry, what happened?"

He hiccupped, rubbing roughly at his eyes. "Father," he managed.

The single word was enough. Eliza scrambled to the corner, prying up the loose board with fingers that suddenly felt numb. The small cloth pouch should have been there, tucked into the shallow space beneath, the pouch containing every penny she'd managed to save over the past three months, including what Jonah had given her after she'd paid for Harry's medicine.

But the space was empty.

"No," she whispered, reaching into the hole as if her savings might materialize if she just felt around enough. "No, no, no."

She flipped the board over, irrationally hoping the pouch had somehow stuck to the underside. Nothing.

"When?" she asked, turning back to Harry. "When did he come home?"

"About an hour after you left," Harry said, his voice small. "I pretended to be asleep. He seemed...he was looking for something. He checked under the mattress first, then the window ledge, and then..." Harry gestured helplessly at the now-empty hiding spot.

"How much did you have hidden?" he asked.

"Almost ten shillings." Three months of saving every spare penny, of going hungry so Harry could eat, of mending clothes by candlelight until her eyes burned. Ten shillings that could have kept them afloat for weeks and they could have used to pay part of the loan. Gone.

The door banged open, and Thomas Tate, swayed in the doorway. His clothes were rumpled, his face flushed with drink. He squinted at Eliza as if trying to bring her into focus.

"There's m'girl," he slurred, taking an unsteady step into the room. "Got any coin for your old da?"

Eliza rose slowly to her feet, something hot and dangerous unfurling in her chest. "Where is it?"

Thomas blinked at her. "Where's what?"

"My money. The savings you stole."

He had the decency to look away, but his shame didn't last. His expression hardened. "Wasn't stealing. Can't steal from your own house."

"That was our money!" Eliza's voice rose sharply. "That was for Harry's medicine, for our rent—"

"And I'm going to double it," Thomas cut in, a sly grin spreading across his face. "Got a hot tip at the card tables. This time tomorrow, we'll have twice as much." He tapped his temple. "Smart thinking, that."

"Smart?" Eliza couldn't believe what she was hearing. "You think gambling our last shillings is smart? The same gambling that's put us in debt to Lockwood?"

Harry coughed from his corner, a harsh, wet sound that seemed to fill the tiny room. Thomas glanced at him, then quickly away.

"You don't understand business opportunities," he muttered. "Woman's mind can't grasp it."

"No, I understand perfectly," Eliza said, stepping closer. "I understand that while I've been working my fingers raw trying to keep us fed and sheltered, you've been drinking away what little you earn and now stealing what isn't yours!"

Thomas drew himself up, swaying slightly. "Watch how you speak to me, girl. I'm still your father."

"Are you?" The words were out before Eliza could stop them. "Because fathers protect their children. They provide. They don't gamble away medicine money while their son coughs himself to death!"

Harry made a small, distressed sound from his corner.

"You think I don't care?" Thomas's face twisted. "You think I like seeing him sick? I'm trying to make things better!"

"By stealing? By gambling? By drinking until you can't stand straight?" Eliza's voice cracked. "Mother would be ashamed of what you've become."

Thomas recoiled as if she'd slapped him. For a moment, he looked truly sober, truly present, and utterly devastated.

"You think I don't know that?" he whispered. His face crumpled, the bluster draining away. "You think I don't see her face every time I close my eyes?" His legs seemed to give out beneath him, and he slid down the wall to sit heavily on the floor. "She was everything good in me."

Eliza stood frozen, unprepared for this sudden vulnerability.

"Every night, I dream she's still here," Thomas continued, his voice barely audible. "And every morning, I wake up and she's gone, and there's only me. Just me, and I'm not enough. I've never been enough without her."

Tears tracked down his unshaven cheeks now, cutting pale paths through the grime. His shoulders began to shake.

"You promised her," Eliza said, her own voice thick with emotion. "Before she died, you promised her you'd take care of us."

Thomas covered his face with hands that trembled. "I know," he sobbed. "God help me, I know."

Harry crawled from his mattress, dragging his blanket with him. He approached his father cautiously, then settled beside him, leaning against Thomas's shoulder.

"I miss her too," Harry whispered.

Thomas's arm came around the boy automatically, pulling him close. For a moment, they looked like what they were meant to be, father and son, united in grief, finding comfort in each other.

Eliza watched them, her anger battling with a deep, unwelcome ache. She wanted to hold onto her rage—it was cleaner, safer than this complicated sorrow. But seeing her father broken open, she glimpsed the man he'd once been: the father who had carried her on his shoulders through London parks, who had taught Harry to whistle, who had looked at their mother like she hung the moon.

She crossed the room and crouched before him. "The money," she said, not unkindly. "Did you spend it all?"

Thomas shook his head, not meeting her eyes. With trembling fingers, he reached into his jacket pocket and pulled out a wrinkled pouch her pouch. He handed it to her.

Eliza opened it, hardly daring to hope. Inside was perhaps a third of what should have been there. The rest, she assumed, had already gone to drink or cards.

"I was going to win it back," Thomas whispered. "I swear it. Was going to come home a hero."

Eliza closed the pouch, her fingers tight around the pathetic remains of their safety net. It wasn't enough, not for rent, not for food for the month, certainly not enough to keep Lockwood's men at bay.

"We can't keep doing this," she said quietly. "Harry needs stability. He needs medicine. He needs..."

"A better father," Thomas finished, his voice hollow.

Eliza didn't contradict him. "He needs the father you used to be," she said instead. "The one who read him stories and taught him to tie his boots."

Thomas looked down at Harry, who had fallen asleep against him, his breathing labored but his face peaceful. With a gentleness Eliza hadn't seen in years, Thomas brushed the hair from his son's forehead.

"I don't know if that man exists anymore," he admitted.

"He does," Eliza said, surprising herself with the certainty in her voice. "He's right there, underneath all that drink and self-pity. The question is whether you want to find him badly enough."

Eliza woke before dawn, her neck stiff from another night on the hard floor. She'd given her thin mattress to Harry, hoping it might help ease his coughing. The medicine had helped some, his fever had broken during the night, but his chest still rattled with each breath.

She moved quietly around their small room,

careful not to wake either Harry or their father. Thomas had eventually fallen asleep in the corner, his face slack and vulnerable in the dim light. Eliza studied him for a moment, searching for traces of the man he'd once been. Sometimes, in sleep, she could almost see him.

The conversation from the night before hung heavy in her mind as she splashed cold water on her face from their cracked basin. They needed money, more than she could earn from ragpicking alone. The coins remaining in her pouch wouldn't stretch far enough, not with Lockwood's men breathing down their necks.

Which meant she had no choice but to follow Jonah Quinn's suggestion.

"Martha Hughes," she whispered to herself as she pulled on her cleanest dress, which wasn't saying much. The fabric was thin from too many washings, and the hem was frayed despite her careful mending. She brushed her hair back from her face and secured it with her mother's old tortoiseshell pin, the only pretty thing she owned.

Harry stirred as she gathered her shawl. "Liza?" he mumbled, blinking up at her. "Where're you going?"

"I might have found work," she whispered,

crouching beside him. "Proper work, with regular pay."

His eyes brightened. "Really? Where?"

"A seamstress shop. The woman who runs it might need help." She pressed her palm to his forehead. It was cool, thank goodness. "I've left bread and cheese on the table for you. Make sure you drink all the tea I've brewed, it has the rest of your medicine in it."

Harry nodded solemnly. "Will you be back soon?"

Eliza hesitated. She had no idea how long this would take, or even if this Martha Hughes would give her the time of day. "I'll try. And if Father wakes...don't tell him where the medicine money is."

Harry's face fell a little. "He was crying last night. After you fell asleep."

"Keep the door locked," she said, ruffling his hair. "And don't let him drag you to the Cock and Bull if he wakes with a thirst."

Eliza wrapped her shawl tighter around her shoulders and headed east, toward the neighborhood Jonah had described.

It took her nearly an hour to find Chapel Street, though she'd been careful to memorize Jonah's directions. The neighborhood wasn't grand, but it was respectable with neat brick buildings with polished door knockers and actual curtains in the windows. Eliza felt suddenly conscious of her worn clothes and calloused hands.

The shop was exactly where Jonah had said it would be: a narrow storefront with "HUGHES DRESSMAKING" painted in elegant gold letters on the window. Through the glass, Eliza could see bolts of fabric in shades she rarely encountered in the East End - rich burgundies, forest greens, and a blue that reminded her of summer skies.

She hesitated on the doorstep. What if this was a mistake? What if Martha Hughes took one look at her and turned her away? What if…

The door swung open, nearly hitting Eliza in the face. A young woman with an armful of packages almost crashed into her.

"Oh! Sorry, love!" the girl exclaimed, steadying herself. "Didn't see you there!"

"My fault," Eliza said, stepping back. "I was just…"

"Were you coming in?" The girl nudged the door wider with her hip. "Go on then. Mrs. Hughes is just setting up."

Before Eliza could respond, the girl was off, hurrying down the street with her parcels. Eliza took a deep breath, squared her shoulders, and stepped inside.

The shop smelled of fresh fabric, beeswax, and something floral, lavender, perhaps. It was tidy but busy, with workbenches along one wall, shelves of thread and notions along another, and bolts of fabric arranged by color on the far wall. A small fitting area occupied one corner, complete with a three-sided mirror.

"Hello?" Eliza called tentatively. "Mrs. Hughes?"

"Just a moment!" came a cheerful voice from the back room. A moment later, a plump woman in her forties emerged, wiping her hands on her apron. She had rosy cheeks, warm brown eyes, and salt-and-pepper hair pinned neatly beneath a lace cap. "Good morning, dear. How can I help you?"

Eliza clasped her hands to keep them from fidgeting. "My name is Eliza Tate. I was told you might be looking for help. With sewing, I mean."

Mrs. Hughes tilted her head, studying Eliza with curious eyes. "Who told you that, if you don't mind my asking?"

"A man named Jonah. Jonah Quinn. He works at the docks."

"Jonah sent you, did he? Well now, that's interesting. He's not one for idle chatter, our Jonah."

Our Jonah? Eliza wondered just how well the seamstress knew him.

"Come, sit down." Mrs. Hughes gestured to a stool near one of the workbenches. "Let's have a proper look at you."

Eliza sat, trying not to hunch her shoulders as the older woman circled her, appraising. She fought the urge to explain her shabby clothes or apologize for her rough hands.

"Have you sewn before, Eliza Tate?" Mrs. Hughes asked.

"Yes, ma'am. I mend clothes, my family's and sometimes others, for a few pence. And I used to help my mother with her work. She was in service at a fine house, and sometimes the ladies would give her their old dresses to alter for herself."

"And did she teach you her skills?"

Eliza nodded. "She showed me how to take in seams, let out hems, turn collars. I can do basic embroidery too, though nothing fancy."

Mrs. Hughes made a thoughtful sound. "Let me see your hands."

Eliza hesitated before holding them out, palms up. They were clean, she'd made sure of that before leaving home but they were worker's hands, the fingertips pricked and callused from years of needlework.

To her surprise, Mrs. Hughes's own hands

weren't much different when she took Eliza's in them. The older woman's palms were soft, but her fingers bore the same telltale marks of someone who'd spent a lifetime with needle and thread.

"Good, strong hands," Mrs. Hughes said approvingly. "Now, can you show me your stitches?"

She produced a scrap of muslin and a needle already threaded with blue silk. Eliza took it, grateful that her hands weren't shaking much. She pulled the thread through the fabric, her stitches small and even, forming a neat row along the edge of the cloth.

Mrs. Hughes watched silently, her head tilted. When Eliza finished and handed the cloth back, the older woman examined it closely.

"Well," she said finally, "your stitches are straighter than Norah's, and she's been with me two years." She looked up at Eliza, her expression softening. "So you need work."

"Yes, ma'am. Very much so."

"Why?"

She could lie, of course. Make up some story about wanting to better herself. But something in Mrs. Hughes's kind face made her opt for honesty instead.

"My brother's sickly," she said quietly. "He needs

medicine, proper food. And our rent's gone up. My father..." She trailed off, not sure how to explain Thomas without sounding disloyal. "My father tries, but he hasn't been the same since my mother passed."

Mrs. Hughes nodded slowly, as if this confirmed something she'd already suspected. "How old are you, Eliza?"

"Twenty, ma'am."

"And carrying the weight of a family on those narrow shoulders," Mrs. Hughes said, more to herself than to Eliza. She straightened, seeming to come to a decision. "Well, as it happens, I am in need of another pair of hands. My business has been growing, I've taken on more clients from the theater, and they always need costumes in a rush."

Hope fluttered in Eliza's chest, but she tamped it down. "I don't know anything about making costumes."

"You'll learn." Mrs. Hughes smiled, and her whole face transformed with it, the corners of her eyes crinkling. "I need someone who can sew a straight line and isn't afraid of hard work. Everything else, I can teach."

Eliza hardly dared believe what she was hearing. "You're offering me a position?"

"I am. Six days a week, Sundays off. Eight in the

morning until six in the evening, with an hour for dinner." Mrs. Hughes named a weekly wage that made Eliza's eyes widen, it was three times what she could hope to make ragpicking. "And I provide tea and bread at midday. Does that suit?"

"Yes," Eliza said, too quickly. "Yes, that would suit very well. Thank you, Mrs. Hughes. You won't regret it."

"Martha, please. Mrs. Hughes makes me feel old." The woman laughed, a hearty sound that filled the small shop. "Now, when can you start? I've a rush order for the Royal Theatre, I've got six shepherdess costumes by Friday."

"Today," Eliza said without hesitation. "Right now, if you'd have me."

Martha looked surprised, but pleased. "Eager, aren't you? Well, I can't say I mind that. Come along, then. Let me show you around properly."

She led Eliza through the shop, explaining the organization of threads and fabrics, introducing her to the two other girls who worked there, Norah, the apprentice, and Betsy, who handled deliveries and simple mending.

"We're like family here," Martha told her as they returned to the main workbench. "I don't tolerate unkindness or gossip. We work hard, but we look after each other." She gave Eliza a significant look. "I hope that suits you."

"It does," Eliza said, meaning it. After years of fighting for scraps and watching her back, the idea of working somewhere with clear rules and expectations felt like luxury.

Martha nodded, satisfied. "Good. Now, let's start you on something simple. These hems need finishing before noon."

She set Eliza up at a workbench by the window, where the morning light streamed in, making it easier to see the fine stitches needed. The work was straightforward but precise, exactly the kind of task Eliza excelled at.

As she fell into the rhythm of the needle, Eliza found herself relaxing just a fraction. The shop was warm, the company pleasant. Norah hummed as she worked across the room, and Martha moved between tables, offering guidance and occasional jokes that made both girls laugh.

For the first time in longer than she could remember, Eliza felt a small spark of hope. This job wouldn't solve her father's drinking, Harry's health, Lockwood's debt but it was a start. A real start.

"You're quick," Martha observed, stopping beside

her an hour later. "And neat. I think you'll do very well here, Eliza Tate."

"Thank you for taking a chance on me," Eliza said, meaning every word.

Martha patted her shoulder. "Thank Jonah Quinn. He doesn't recommend people lightly." She hesitated, then added more softly, "He's a good man, whatever his secrets."

Before Eliza could ask what she meant by that, Martha was moving on, calling to Norah about a missing pattern. Eliza turned back to her work, thoughts whirling. What did Martha know about Jonah that she didn't? And why had he gone out of his way to help her?

Questions for another time. For now, she had work to do. A real work, with real pay. And for the first time in months, Eliza allowed herself to imagine a future where Harry might have medicine regularly, where they might have enough to eat, where they might even find a better room, away from the drafts that made her brother's cough worse.

It wasn't everything, but it was something. And something, Eliza had learned long ago, was a start.

CHAPTER 6

Jonah pressed his back against the damp brick wall of the alley, the bitter taste of fear coating his tongue. He'd been watching the docks for nearly an hour now, and his muscles were stiff from holding the same position. Everything he has built for 5 years was now it was crumbling beneath his feet because he'd hesitated too long.

Because of a girl. He pulled his cap lower, staying in the shadows as dock workers trudged past, unaware of his presence. The evening mist rolling in from the Thames provided additional cover, but it wouldn't matter if Silas had already recognized him.

That moment in the warehouse still replayed in his mind. The way Silas's eyes had narrowed, tilting his slightly as if trying to place a half-remembered face.

Jonah had bolted then, even though Silas instructed him to wait. By now, Silas would have had time to remember exactly who he was, the apprentice who should have been transported, who should have died in the Thames current five years ago.

A seagull shrieked overhead, making him flinch. Stay or run? The sensible choice was obvious. He had enough saved to start again somewhere in Liverpool, perhaps, or even Bristol. Somewhere Lockwood's reach couldn't extend.

But something, someone kept him rooted to London's filthy streets.

Movement near the customs office caught his eye. Silas Grady, looking far too polished for the grimy docklands, was deep in conversation with one of the customs officers. Jonah recognized Peterson, a man known to accept bribes in exchange for looking the other way when certain shipments needed to bypass proper inspection.

He strained to hear their conversation, inching closer along the wall.

"...Lockwood wants the shipment expedited," Silas was saying, his voice carrying on the evening air. "Can't have it sitting in your warehouse gathering dust."

Peterson nodded eagerly. "Of course, Mr. Grady. We understand the urgency. The textile mill is expecting delivery by…"

"Friday. Not a day later." Silas handed over what appeared to be a small envelope. "The mill up north is expanding operations. Mr. Lockwood has invested considerably in the machinery."

"And the, ah… labor arrangements?" Peterson asked, tucking the envelope into his coat with practiced quickness.

Silas's thin lips curved into what might generously be called a smile. "Being handled as we speak. It's amazing how many families are eager to put their children to work these days."

Jonah's hands curled into fists. He knew exactly what kind of "labor arrangements" Lockwood preferred, children as young as six or seven, working fourteen-hour days for pennies, tiny hands perfect for reaching into dangerous machinery.

"Jonah? Christ, man, I thought that was you."

The voice behind him nearly stopped his heart. Jonah spun around to find Collin, a fellow dockworker who'd shared drinks with him once or twice at the Anchor.

"Bit suspicious, lurking in alleys," Collin said with a grin that revealed a missing front tooth. "Watching the customs men, are we?"

"Just catching my breath," Jonah muttered, glancing back toward Silas, who was still occupied with Peterson.

"Haven't seen you loading today," Collin continued, oblivious to Jonah's tension. "Foreman's been asking after you. Said there's extra work if you want it this week."

"Is that so?" Jonah replied, trying to appear casual.

Collin nodded, leaning against the wall. "Aye. That Lockwood fellow's been increasing shipments to his factories. Textiles, mostly. Heard he's opening another mill up north." He scratched his beard. "Means they'll be needing more hands, of course."

"More children, you mean," Jonah said, unable to keep the bitterness from his voice.

Collin shrugged. "It's how it's always been. Lockwood's putting out word he needs another thirty boys for the new operation. Small ones, eight to ten years old." His voice lowered. "Heard that snake Grady's been making rounds in the East End, offering families a few shillings to sign their boys away."

Jonah had never met Eliza's brother but he'd be the perfect age for Lockwood's mills.

"Terrible business," Collin continued. "Lost my youngest brother to a mill like that. His arm got caught in the machinery." He made a sharp gesture. "Gone, just like that. Boss sent him home without a penny, said it was the boy's fault for being careless."

Jonah barely heard him. If Lockwood was sending recruiters to the East End, it was only a matter of time before they reached Eliza's neighborhood. With her father deep in debt to Lockwood, they'd be prime targets.

"You alright, mate? Look like you've seen a ghost," Collin said, peering at him.

"Fine," Jonah managed. "Just remembered something I need to do."

Collin clapped him on the shoulder. "Well, if you want that work, better show up tomorrow. Good money, if you don't mind loading Lockwood's crates."

As Collin ambled away, Jonah remained frozen in place. This changed everything. It wasn't just about him anymore, or even just about helping Eliza with a few coins. If Lockwood and Grady were expanding their operations, countless children would be swept into their factories. Children like Harry.

He glanced back toward the customs house. Silas was gone, but the implications of what he'd overhead remained. A shipment of textiles headed north, a new mill opening, and a need for small hands to operate the machinery.

The sensible choice would be to vanish tonight. Take his savings, board the first coach out of London, and never look back.

Five years ago, he'd saved himself and no one else. He'd escaped Lockwood's trap while others, younger apprentices, and children on that same shop with him had remained behind to suffer. He'd told himself there was nothing he could have done, that one man couldn't fight someone like Augustus Lockwood.

Now he wasn't so sure.

He pushed away from the wall. He would need to be careful, more careful than ever before. Silas was already suspicious, and if Lockwood discovered Jonah Quinn was still alive, still in London...

But he couldn't run. Not yet.

First, he needed to warn Eliza about what was coming. And then, perhaps, there was something more he could do to stop Lockwood's shipment, or to disrupt the machinery that ground children's lives to dust for profit.

It was madness, of course. One man against Augustus Lockwood's empire.

Jonah trudged back to the shed, running through different plans and possibilities, none of them particularly good. The night air had grown colder, and his breath formed small clouds as he picked his way through the maze of crates and barrels that lined the path to his temporary lodging.

He'd have to find new shelter soon. This shed was too close to the docks, too close to where Silas had almost recognized him. Perhaps he could find a room in another one of the boarding houses on the outskirts of the city, not too far from the East End, but far enough from the docks to avoid immediate detection.

The wooden door creaked as he pushed it open, and he froze at the sight of a figure waiting inside.

"Eliza?" His voice came out rougher than intended, surprise mingling with a sudden, irrational flare of panic. Had something happened? Had Grady already come for Harry?

She stood quickly from the upturned crate she'd been sitting on, her cheeks flushed from the cold or perhaps from running. Her dark hair was coming loose from its pins, and her eyes, those striking blue eyes were bright in the dim light filtering through the shed's single grimy window.

"I'm sorry for coming unannounced," she said, breathless. "I wasn't sure you'd still be here."

Jonah glanced past her to where his small pack sat in the corner, already half-filled with his meager possessions. The coins he'd planned to take with him were tucked into the hidden pocket he'd sewn into his coat lining.

"I'm still here," he said, closing the door behind him and shoving his hands into his pockets to warm them. "Is everything... is Harry alright?"

Eliza nodded, the tension in her shoulders easing slightly. "He's better. The medicine you gave me money for helped a lot. His breathing's easier now." She hesitated, twisting her hands together. "That's... that's part of why I came. To thank you properly."

Jonah shifted uncomfortably. He wasn't accustomed to gratitude. "No need," he muttered, moving toward the small pot-bellied stove in the corner. There were still a few coals glowing inside, and he added a handful from the bucket beside it. The shed was hardly luxurious, but at least it kept out the worst of the wind.

"There is a need," Eliza insisted, "You didn't have

to help us. Most people wouldn't have." She paused. "My father took some of my money."

"What?" Jonah turned to face her.

"He stole my savings, nearly ten shillings I'd been putting away." There was a tightness to her expression, but no tears. "I'd hidden it under a floorboard, but he found it. He gambled them away."

Jonah cursed under his breath. "All of it?"

"No. He left some. Enough for Harry's medicine, at least." She tucked a loose strand of hair behind her ear, a ghost of a smile touching her lips. "He's... promised to stop drinking. I don't know if he means it this time, but he seemed different. Broken, but maybe in a way that might finally let him put himself back together."

Jonah didn't know what to say to that. In his experience, men who drank to escape rarely found their way back. But there was something in Eliza's voice that made him reluctant to voice his skepticism.

"I went to see Martha Hughes," she continued, brightening visibly. "You were right about her. She's given me work sewing for her shop. The pay is good, better than I'd get anywhere else with my skills."

"That's good," Jonah said, genuinely pleased for her. "Martha's fair. She won't cheat you."

"I can afford Harry's medicine now. Food too, proper food, not just scraps." Eliza's eyes almost glittered in the dim light of the shed. "Maybe even move to better lodgings eventually. Somewhere drier, with a stove."

Jonah watched her as she spoke, struck by the animation in her face. Something that made it hard to look away. The thought of not hearing her voice again caused an unexpected ache in his chest.

Eliza took a step toward him, then another, until she stood close enough that he could see the faint freckles across her nose, nearly invisible in the dim lamplight.

"So do you," she said quietly.

Before he could respond, she reached out and took his hand in both of hers. Her fingers were cold but surprisingly strong, calloused from years of work.

"Don't leave London," she said, the words somewhere between a command and a plea.

Jonah stared down at their joined hands, then at her upturned face. "It's complicated."

"It always is," she replied. "But you helped me when you didn't have to. And Martha says..." she trailed off.

"What did Martha say?" he asked, suddenly alert.

"That you're a good man who's had bad luck." Eliza squeezed his hand. "She wouldn't tell me more, said it wasn't her story to share."

Martha knew more than she should about his past, but she'd always been discreet.

Yet looking at Eliza's face, Jonah made a decision that went against every survival instinct he'd honed.

"I'm not leaving," he said.

Her smile bloomed, genuine and bright. "Good."

"For now," he added, needing to be clear. "But Eliza, there are things you don't know about me, about why it might be safer for everyone if I did leave."

"Everyone has secrets," she said simply. "I'm not asking for yours. Just..." she hesitated, then pressed on. "Just don't disappear without saying goodbye."

The simplicity of her request caught him off guard. Not demands for explanations or promises he couldn't keep, just the basic courtesy of a farewell.

"I can manage that," he said.

She released his hand and stepped back, a faint blush coloring her cheeks as if she'd just realized the boldness of her actions. "I'll bring meals, like I promised. My payment for your help."

Jonah hesitated, uncomfortable with the idea of

taking anything more from her. "You don't need to bring me meals. You've got your brother to feed."

"I insist," Eliza said, straightening her shoulders with surprising stubbornness. "Is it because my cooking is tasteless? I'm not the best cook, but I can manage a decent stew."

"No, it's not that at all," Jonah said quickly. In fact, he couldn't remember the last time he'd had a home-cooked meal rather than whatever cheap fare he could grab from street vendors and what she brought him.

"What is it then?" Her blue eyes challenged him directly.

Jonah sighed, running a hand through his hair. "I just... I couldn't possibly take from the little you have. You need every penny for Harry, for your new lodgings."

"And I need to pay my debts," Eliza countered. "You helped me when no one else would. I'd be offended if you didn't accept it."

Her chin jutted forward in a way that suggested further argument would be pointless. Jonah had faced down angry dockmasters and survived five years in hiding, but something about this small, fierce woman made him want to surrender.

"Fine," he conceded, lips quirking into what felt

like his first genuine smile in days. "I accept. Thank you."

Eliza nodded, clearly satisfied with her victory. She paused, studying his face. "Why are you running away, Jonah? What are you afraid of?"

The question hung between them. Jonah turned away, busying himself with adjusting the damper on the stove. The old instinct to deflect, to hide, rose within him.

"I'm sorry," Eliza said quietly after his silence stretched too long. "I shouldn't pry. It's none of my business."

"It's nothing," Jonah said automatically, then stopped himself. For some inexplicable reason, he didn't want to lie to her. Perhaps it was because she'd been honest with him, or perhaps it was simply that he was tired of carrying his secrets alone.

"Lockwood," he said finally, the name feeling like rust in his mouth. "That's what I'm afraid of."

Eliza's eyes widened. "Augustus Lockwood? The merchant?"

"The same." Jonah moved to the small window, checking the darkness outside. Old habits. "I used to work for him, years ago. Before the docks."

"As what?"

"A cooper's apprentice." He touched his callused

hands together, remembering the feel of shaping wood instead of hauling crates. "I was good at it. Had just made my first proper drinking cup. My master said I had the makings of a fine journeyman."

"What happened?" Eliza asked quietly.

Jonah took a deep breath. The story had lived inside him for so long, never spoken aloud, that the words felt strange on his tongue.

"Lockwood accused me of stealing from his warehouse. Said I'd taken valuable goods that were missing from a shipment." He shook his head. "I never took a thing. But Lockwood had influence and money. So on one questioned him."

"That's terrible."

"It gets worse," Jonah said, leaning against the wall. "I was sentenced to transportation. To Australia." He watched her face pale in the dim light. "Seven years, minimum. More likely I'd never return."

"Oh my God!" Eliza whispered.

"The night before I was to be transported, I escaped. Ran to the Thames." He could still feel the cold air searing his lungs as he fled through the dark streets. "I jumped in. I preferred to be dead than be transported."

"You faked your death," she said

Jonah nodded. "The river's current nearly finished the job properly. But I survived." He coughed slightly. "I've been hiding ever since. Changed my appearance, took work at the docks where nobody asks questions. But I kept my real name, Jonah Quinn. No one would connect a dead cooper's apprentice to a dock worker."

"And now Lockwood's back," Eliza said.

"He never left. I just avoided him successfully until now." Jonah ran a hand through his hair. "He was at the docks with his man Silas Grady. I think Grady almost recognized me. And there's a customs inspector asking questions about my past."

"That's why you were planning to leave," she said, her eyes falling on his half-packed bag in the corner.

"I should have gone as soon as I heard Lockwood was in town" Jonah admitted. "I would have, but..."

He stopped, the words catching in his throat as he realized what he was about to say.

Eliza stepped closer, "But what?"

Jonah looked away, unable to meet her gaze. "I couldn't."

"Was it because of me?" she asked

. He remained silent, staring at the glowing coals in the small stove.

Eliza's smile grew slowly, lighting up her face

even in the dim shed. "I'm glad," she said simply. "I'm glad you stayed, whatever the reason."

Something unfamiliar and warm unfurled in Jonah's chest at her words. It had been so long since anyone had been glad of his presence.

"What will you do now?" she asked. "You can't keep hiding forever."

"I'm not sure," he admitted, then surprised himself with what he said next. "I want to stop him, Eliza. Lockwood is expanding his operations, opening more mills up north. He's sending Grady to the East End to recruit more children."

"Children?," Eliza said, her expression hardening.

"Yes. Collin, another dock worker told me Lockwood's looking for thirty boys, ages eight to ten." He spat the words. "I've seen what happens in those mills. Children will be worked until they drop, or worse lose their limbs to the machines."

"We have to stop him," Eliza said, her voice fierce.

Jonah's head snapped up. "We? No. This isn't your fight."

"It is if he's coming for children in my neighborhood," she countered. "My brother could be the next victim."

"Eliza, you don't understand. Lockwood is

dangerous. Powerful. He has men like Grady to do his dirty work. I can't ask you to risk yourself—"

"You're not asking. I'm offering." Her chin lifted in that stubborn way he was starting to recognize. "I'll help you. Whatever you're planning."

"I can't involve you in this," Jonah insisted.

"We're friends now, aren't we?" Eliza said, as if it were the simplest thing in the world. "And friends fight for each other."

Friends. The word caught him off guard. When was the last time anyone had claimed friendship with him?

"Is that why you're here without a chaperone?" he asked, a hint of teasing slipping into his voice despite himself. "Visiting a man alone at night? Some might say that's beyond friendship."

Eliza's cheeks flushed scarlet, visible even in the dim light. "I—I should go. Harry will be worried if he wakes and finds me gone."

She moved toward the door quickly, clearly flustered, but Jonah caught her arm gently.

"Let me walk you back to the main road, at least," he said. "It's not safe this late."

She nodded, not quite meeting his eyes. "Thank you."

They walked in silence through the maze of

crates and barrels, Jonah alert to any sound or movement that might signal trouble. The docks were never truly deserted, even at this hour, but the area near his shed was quiet enough. When they reached the lamp-lit street that would lead her back toward Spitalfields, Jonah stopped.

"Be careful," he said. "And think about what I've said. Lockwood isn't someone to cross lightly."

"I will," Eliza promised. She hesitated, then added, "Come to Martha's shop tomorrow if you can. We can talk more there."

Jonah nodded, watching as she hurried away, her slim figure soon swallowed by the darkness between street lamps.

He turned back toward his shed, mind churning with thoughts he couldn't quiet. For five years, he'd thought only of survival, of staying hidden, of avoiding the past that threatened to drag him under. Every decision had been made with one purpose: self-preservation.

Now, walking back through the silent docks, Jonah realized something had fundamentally shifted. He hadn't left London not just because he needed to warn Eliza about Lockwood's plans, but because for the first time in years, he had something—someone—he wanted to protect.

The realization should have terrified him. Attachment meant vulnerability, and vulnerability meant danger. But as he slipped back into the cold shed, Jonah found himself planning not for escape, but for a confrontation that had been five years in the making.

CHAPTER 7

"What's that smile about, then? Got a sweetheart hiding somewhere?"

Eliza's head snapped up from the ivory silk she'd been meticulously stitching. Penny, one of Martha's younger apprentices, was watching her with a mischievous grin.

"I don't know what you're talking about," Eliza said, focusing back on her work, willing the heat in her cheeks to subside.

"Oh, come off it. You've been smiling at nothing all morning. Like..."

"Like what?" Eliza tried to keep her tone neutral, but even she could hear the defensive edge.

"Like you're seeing something the rest of us can't." Penny leaned closer, lowering her voice conspiratorially. "Is it that butcher's boy? I've seen him watching you when you pass the shop."

Eliza rolled her eyes. "I've got more important things to think about than boys."

But even as she said it, Jonah's face flashed in her mind—that rare smile breaking through his guarded expression, the way his eyes had softened when she'd insisted on bringing him food. The memory sent an unwelcome flutter through her stomach.

"Your face is telling a different story," Martha called from across the room, not looking up from the bodice she was cutting. "You're red as a February robin."

The other girls giggled, and Eliza sighed, jabbing her needle through the delicate fabric with perhaps more force than necessary.

"It's nothing like that," she insisted, though the words felt like a lie on her tongue. She couldn't deny the pull she felt toward Jonah, the way her heart had raced when he'd teased her about visiting his shed unchaperoned. But attraction was a luxury she couldn't afford, not with Harry to care for and Lockwood's debt hanging over them.

"If you say so," Penny sing-songed, returning to her work.

Eliza bent her head over the dress again, a

commission for a merchant's daughter's wedding. The silk was the finest material she'd ever handled, slipping like water between her fingers. Martha had trusted her with the delicate work after seeing her skill with the needle, and Eliza was determined not to disappoint.

For the next few hours, she lost herself in the rhythm of stitching, grateful that the work kept her mind from wandering to Jonah or worrying about Harry, who'd seemed stronger this morning before she left.

"Finished," she announced finally, holding up the completed bodice for Martha's inspection. The older woman examined it critically, turning it over in her hands.

"Excellent work, Eliza. Your stitches are nearly invisible." Martha nodded approvingly. "I'll have you start on the sleeves tomorrow. For now, that's enough for today."

She reached into her pocket and counted out coins into Eliza's palm. "One shilling and sixpence."

Eliza stared at the money. It was more than she'd ever earned in a single day. Enough for Harry's medicine for weeks, with some left over for food and toward their rent. A small fortune compared to what she'd made ragpicking.

"Thank you," she said, clutching the coins tightly.

"You've earned it," Martha replied, already turning to examine another girl's work. "Be here at six tomorrow."

The late afternoon sun cast long shadows as Eliza headed home, her step lighter than it had been in years. The weight of the coins in her pocket felt like promise, like possibility. Perhaps they could move to a better room eventually, one where Harry wouldn't wheeze from the damp. Perhaps she could even save for that sewing machine.

Her good mood evaporated the moment she pushed open their door.

Thomas lay sprawled on the floor, one eye swollen shut, dried blood crusting his nostrils and split lip. The room was in disarray, the few possessions they owned scattered as if someone had searched through them.

"Father!" Eliza dropped to her knees beside him, checking for signs of life. His chest rose and fell unevenly, and the stench of gin hung heavy around him.

His good eye fluttered open at her touch. "Liza..."

"What happened?" she demanded, scanning the room. "Where's Harry?"

Thomas made a choked sound, somewhere between a groan and a sob.

"Where is Harry?" Eliza repeated, panic rising in her throat.

"Gone," Thomas croaked. "Silas took him."

Her blood froze. "What do you mean, Silas took him? Took him where?"

Thomas's face crumpled, tears cutting tracks through the grime on his cheeks. "For the loan. Said we'd... we'd had our chances."

"But I gave you money!" Eliza gripped his shirt, shaking him slightly. "I gave you that money to pay back Lockwood!"

"I thought..." Thomas coughed, wincing. "Thought I could double it. At the gaming tables. Just needed a bit of luck..."

"You gambled Harry's future away?"

"It'll only be for a year or two," Thomas whispered, not meeting her eyes. "Lockwood's sending him to work at one of his mills up north. Said he'd cancel the debt..."

"A year or two?" Eliza's voice rose to a shout. "Do you know what happens to children in those mills? How many don't come back at all?"

Thomas said nothing, tears flowing freely now.

"I trusted you," she said, each word sharp as glass.

"I trusted you after that day. You said you were going to be honest and get a job."

"I'm sorry, Liza…"

"Don't." She stood up, backing away from him as if he were something poisonous. "Don't you dare apologize now. It's too late."

She paced the small room, mind racing. "When did they take him? How long ago?"

"This morning. After you left for work."

"All day," she whispered, horror washing through her. "He's been gone all day and you've been here, drinking?"

"I tried to stop them, Liza. Silas did this." Thomas gestured weakly at his battered face.

"And then you crawled to the gin bottle instead of coming to find me?" The rage that had been building exploded out of her. "I don't want to ever see you again."

"Eliza, please…"

"If anything happens to Harry, anything, I'll never forgive you. Do you understand me? I'll hate you for the rest of my life."

Thomas reached for her hand, but she jerked away.

"I wish it had been you," she said, her voice

breaking. "I wish you had died instead of Mother. She would never have let this happen."

The words hung between them like a physical thing. Thomas recoiled as if she'd struck him, his face crumpling with grief and shame.

Eliza couldn't bear to look at him anymore. She grabbed her shawl and headed for the door.

"Where are you going?" Thomas called weakly.

"To find my brother," she said, not turning back. "Don't be here when I return."

She slammed the door behind her and ran down the stairs, tears blurring her vision. Once outside, she leaned against the building, trying to compose herself. Panic wouldn't help Harry.

Lockwood. She needed to find Lockwood, or Silas. Or Jonah. Jonah would know what to do, where to look.

She wiped the tears from her face with her sleeve and set off toward the docks. She would find Harry if she had to tear all of London apart with her bare hands.

Eliza flew through the streets. East London's maze of alleys and byways had never seemed so vast, so impenetrable. Every second that passed was another moment Harry was further from her reach.

The evening crowds thickened as workers

streamed home, blocking her path and slowing her frantic pace. She pushed through, ignoring the curses and shouts that followed in her wake.

"Watch where you're going, girl!"

"What's the fire, then?"

She didn't have time to explain, didn't have time to apologize. Harry needed her. That was all that mattered.

Her lungs burned by the time she reached Mrs. Burrows' corner shop, the old woman sweeping the doorstep as she did every evening before closing.

"Mrs. Burrows!" Eliza called, her voice ragged.

The shopkeeper looked up, frowning at Eliza's disheveled appearance. "Goodness, child, what's happened to you?"

"Have you seen Harry?" Eliza grabbed the woman's arm, not caring how desperate she appeared. "My brother. Have you seen him today?"

Mrs. Burrows' expression shifted from annoyance to concern. "Not since yesterday when he came for a ha'penny worth of licorice. Why? What's happened?"

"He's been taken." The words caught in Eliza's throat. "A man named Silas took him."

Understanding darkened the older woman's face. "Silas Grady? Augustus Lockwood's man?"

Eliza nodded, hope flaring. "You know him?"

"Everyone knows to stay clear of that one." Mrs. Burrows shook her head. "Cruel as they come, that Grady. If he's taken your Harry, it'll be to one of Lockwood's places."

"Do you know where? Please, Mrs. Burrows, anything you know could help."

"Can't say for certain." The woman's brow furrowed. "But Lockwood has a warehouse near the riverside where they sometimes hold people before shipping them north."

"Which warehouse?" Eliza's fingers dug into Mrs. Burrows' sleeve.

"I don't know, child." She gently extracted herself from Eliza's grip. "But Jenkins might. He delivers coal all over that area."

Without waiting for more, Eliza was off again, racing toward Jenkins' small yard where the coal merchant kept his cart. But the yard was locked, the windows of his small office dark. Too late. He'd already gone home for the day.

Eliza slammed her palm against the wooden gate in frustration, ignoring the sting. She couldn't wait until morning. By then, Harry could be on a transport heading north, beyond her reach forever.

"Looking for Jenkins?"

Eliza whirled around to find a man watching her from across the street, a clay pipe dangling from his mouth.

"Yes! Do you know where he is?"

The man shrugged. "Pub, most likely. The Black Swan on Cheapside."

Eliza didn't thank him, already halfway down the street, her shoes slapping against the cobblestones. The Black Swan was packed when she arrived, the air thick with tobacco smoke and the smell of spilled beer. She scanned the crowded room, searching for Jenkins' stooped figure among the drinkers.

She spotted him at a corner table, deep in his cups, a half-empty pint before him.

"Mr. Jenkins!"

The coal merchant squinted up at her. "Do I know you, girl?"

"I need your help." Eliza didn't bother with pleasantries. "Mrs. Burrows said you might know about a warehouse, one where Augustus Lockwood might be keeping children before sending them north."

Jenkins' watery eyes widened, and he glanced nervously around the pub. "Keep your voice down," he hissed. "That's not the sort of thing one discusses openly."

"My brother's been taken," Eliza said, dropping her voice but refusing to back down. "Please."

Something in her face must have moved him, because Jenkins sighed and leaned forward. "There's a warehouse near Wapping. Number Eight, gray stone, Lockwood's name over the entrance. But you'd be a fool to go there. Grady keeps men posted."

"Thank you," Eliza breathed, already backing away.

"Wait!" Jenkins called after her. "I saw something this morning. Might be nothing, but there was a wagon, near St. Katharine's Dock. Had a boy in it, fighting something fierce. Small lad, dark hair."

Eliza's heart stuttered. "Did you see where they took him?"

"Not exactly." Jenkins scratched his stubbled chin. "But I heard one of the men mention Warehouse Four. Said something about the ship not being ready yet."

"Warehouse Four. At St. Katharine's Dock?" Eliza confirmed, her pulse quickening.

Jenkins nodded. "But girl, if that's your brother, you won't get him out alone. Lockwood's men are—"

But Eliza was already gone, pushing her way back through the crowded pub and into the night air. St. Katharine's Dock. She knew where that was.

Jonah had mentioned Warehouse Four before, it was where he'd told her to find the mill ends that had earned her six precious pence.

Jonah. She needed Jonah.

The streets blurred beneath her feet as she ran toward the docks, trying to remember the exact path to Jonah's shed. Twice she took a wrong turn, cursing as she backtracked, precious minutes slipping away. The dockyard was eerily quiet at this hour, most of the day workers gone, the night watchmen not yet making their rounds.

Finally, she spotted the small wooden structure tucked between larger warehouse buildings. Light flickered behind its single dirty window. Jonah was there.

Eliza pounded on the door with her fist, gasping for breath, her sides aching from running.

"Jonah!" Her voice cracked, desperation making it sharp. "Jonah, please!"

The door swung open suddenly, and she nearly fell forward. Jonah caught her by the shoulders, his expression alarmed.

"Eliza? What's happened?"

She clutched at his shirt, struggling to catch her breath. "It's Harry. Silas took Harry."

Jonah's face hardened, his grip on her arms tightening. "When? How?"

"This morning." The words tumbled out between ragged breaths. "My father—he gambled away the money I gave him. The money you gave me. He was supposed to pay Lockwood, but instead—" Her voice broke. "Silas came and took Harry to work in one of Lockwood's northern mills."

Jonah pulled her inside the shed, closing the door quickly behind them. The small space was warm from the stove, the air close.

"Did you see where they took him? Any idea at all?"

"Jenkins, the coal merchant, said he saw a boy—he thinks it was Harry—being taken to Warehouse Four at St. Katharine's Dock." Eliza's fingers dug into Jonah's arms. "He said they mentioned something about a ship not being ready yet."

Something flickered across Jonah's face—recognition, maybe even hope.

"Warehouse Four," he repeated, almost to himself. "The northern shipment."

"Do you know it?" Eliza searched his face. "Jonah, please. I have to find him. Harry's not strong enough for mill work. It'll kill him."

"I know." Jonah's voice was grim. "I've seen what happens to children in those places."

"Then help me," Eliza pleaded. "I can't do this alone."

"Please," she whispered. "He's all I have."

CHAPTER 8

Jonah stared at Eliza, his mind racing. Her brother—taken. The northern mills. He knew what happened there. Small fingers caught in machinery. Limbs mangled. Children worked until they dropped.

"We'll find him," he said, his voice steadier than he felt. "But we need to move fast. Dawn shipments leave early."

Eliza's eyes, still glazed with tears, fixed on his face. "You know where they're keeping him?"

"The warehouses are sorted by shipping route. Four is primarily northern goods." He grabbed his coat from the nail by the door. "I need to get information first, exact details about when and where they're taking him."

"How?"

"The foreman keeps all the shipping manifests. He'll have the records on any transport arranged by Lockwood."

Jonah checked his pocket. Three shillings and fourpence—nearly everything he had. He'd been saving for his escape, but now... He tucked the coins back into his pocket, grabbed a worn cap and pulled it low over his eyes.

"Wait here," he told Eliza. "If anyone knocks, don't answer. I'll be back within the hour."

"I'm coming with you," she said immediately, straightening her shoulders.

"No. The docks at night are no place for—"

"For a woman?" Her eyes flashed. "My brother is out there. I'm not sitting here waiting."

Jonah ran a hand through his hair. He didn't have time to argue. "Fine. But stay close and don't speak to anyone."

The docks were quieter at night but never truly still. Lanterns hung from posts, casting yellow pools across the wooden planking. Night watchmen patrolled between stacks of crates. Dockhands loaded late shipments by lamplight.

Jonah led Eliza through the shadows, avoiding

the patrolling guards. He knew every blind spot, and pattern of the watchmen.

"The foreman's office is there," Jonah whispered, pointing to a small shack raised on stilts over the water. Light leaked from its windows. "Wait behind those barrels."

"What are you going to do?"

"Whatever I have to."

He approached the office, not bothering to hide himself now. The wooden steps creaked under his weight. He knocked once and entered without waiting for an answer.

Foreman Miller sat at his desk, a gas lamp illuminating the papers spread before him and his half-empty bottle of gin. He looked up with bloodshot eyes.

"Quinn? What the hell do you want at this hour?"

Jonah shut the door behind him. "Information."

Miller's expression hardened. "I'm not in the business of—"

"Two shillings." Jonah placed the coins on the desk between them. "For Lockwood's shipment details."

The foreman's eyes darted to the money, then back to Jonah's face. "Lockwood? You know better than to mess with his business."

"I'm not messing with anything. Just need to know what's going where."

Miller's fingers tapped on his desk. "Why?"

"Does it matter for two shillings?"

The foreman picked up one of the coins, testing its weight between his fingers. After a moment, he pocketed both.

"What specifically are you looking for?"

"Children. Being shipped north. Today or tomorrow."

Something flashed across Miller's face, discomfort, maybe even guilt. He shuffled through his papers, pulled one out, and studied it.

"Nothing on the regular manifests. Lockwood runs clean books here." He hesitated, then opened a drawer and extracted a leather-bound ledger. "But there's a private carriage arranged for dawn tomorrow. Listed as 'unregistered cargo' for a textile mill in Lancashire."

"Unregistered cargo," Jonah repeated, his jaw clenching.

Miller avoided his eyes. "That's all I know. Carriage leaves from Warehouse Four, first light." He raised his gaze. "You didn't hear it from me."

Jonah nodded. "One other thing, what is the quickest way to intercept once they're on the road?"

Miller's brow furrowed. "You planning something stupid, Quinn?"

"I need the information only."

The foreman sighed. "Northern road out of London. They'll take the turnpike through Highgate. Only route that makes sense for a carriage." He took a swig of gin. "Now get out before someone sees you here."

Jonah found Eliza exactly where he'd left her, crouched behind the barrels.

"Harry's being moved at dawn," he told her in a low voice. "Private carriage not officially registered on the shipping documents."

"Where are they taking him?"

"Lancashire mill." He guided her away from the docks, back toward his shed. "We have until morning, but we need more than just the two of us to stop a carriage."

"What about the constables?" Eliza asked.

Jonah gave a bitter laugh. "They're paid to look the other way. And we have no proof Lockwood's doing anything illegal. Child labor's perfectly legal in the mills."

"Then what do we do?"

"I know someone who might help. But it'll cost me."

Back in his shed, Jonah lifted a loose floorboard and removed a small metal box. He opened it, revealing his meager treasures: a shilling, two pennies, and a gold pocket watch. He held up the watch, its chain dangling in the lamplight.

"Last thing of value I have."

Eliza's eyes widened. "Is that real gold?"

"It was my father's." He tucked it into his pocket. "There's a man called Morgan who deals in information. If anyone knows the details of Lockwood's routes and weaknesses, it's him."

"Can we trust him?"

"No." Jonah met her eyes directly. "But he'll sell anything to anyone for the right price."

The streets grew darker and quieter as they moved away from the docks, twisting through narrow alleys where refuse piled against walls. Jonah moved with purpose, guiding Eliza through a maze that would confuse most Londoners.

They stopped before a faded green door set into a brick wall. No sign marked the establishment. Jonah knocked three times, paused, then twice more.

A small panel in the door slid open, revealing suspicious eyes.

"Business?" a gruff voice demanded.

"I need to see Morgan. Tell him it's about Lockwood's special shipments."

The eyes narrowed, then the panel slammed shut. A moment later, the door opened.

The interior was dimly lit, smoke hanging in the air. A handful of rough-looking men sat at scattered tables, drinking and speaking in hushed tones. Jonah steered Eliza through the room, ignoring the stares that followed them.

In the back corner sat a thin man with a waxed mustache and spectacles that glinted in the lamplight. He looked more like a clerk than the information broker Jonah knew him to be.

"Quinn." Morgan's voice was higher than his appearance suggested. "Unexpected. And with company, no less."

"I need information, Morgan."

"You know my information has a price."

Jonah took out the pocket watch, dangling it between them. Morgan's eyes fixed on it immediately, a small smile forming beneath his mustache.

"Fourteen-carat gold, if I'm not mistaken."

"Lockwood's moving children north. Shipping out at dawn in a private carriage."

Morgan leaned back, folding his hands on the table. "And you'd like to know...?"

"The exact route. Where to intercept and number of guards he'll have."

"Planning something heroic, Quinn? Not like you to stick your neck out." Morgan's gaze shifted to Eliza, understanding dawning in his eyes. "Ah. Personal interest, is it?"

"The watch," Jonah said flatly. "Take it or leave it."

Morgan plucked the watch from Jonah's fingers, examining it in the light. He popped the case open, checked the mechanism, then snapped it shut with a satisfied nod.

"Lockwood's carriage will take the northern road through Highgate, as expected." He lowered his voice. "But there's a spot just past the Three-Mile marker where the road narrows between two hills. Trees on both sides. Good place for an... intervention."

"Guards?" Jonah pressed.

"Driver and two men. Armed, but nothing heavy but pistols, most likely." Morgan smiled thinly. "Lockwood doesn't want to draw attention with too much security. Might make people wonder what he's transporting."

"What time will they reach that point?"

"Leave at dawn, they'll hit the narrows by seven, assuming no delays." Morgan pocketed the watch.

"I'd imagine you'd want to be in position well before that."

Jonah nodded, preparing to stand.

"Well, good luck with your... rescue mission. I'd hate to hear you drowned in the Thames. Again."

Jonah stood, pulling Eliza with him. "Appreciate the information."

"Always a pleasure doing business." Morgan raised his glass in a mock toast. "Oh, and Quinn? I'd leave London after this. Permanently."

Outside, Eliza gripped Jonah's arm. "What did he mean about drowning? About ghosts?"

"He knows who I really am." Jonah kept walking, increasing his pace. "And if Morgan knows, others might too."

"Will he tell Lockwood?"

"Not tonight. He's already got what he wanted." Jonah patted his empty pocket where the watch had been. "But tomorrow? Next week? Morgan sells to the highest bidder."

"I'm sorry about your watch," Eliza said quietly.

"It's just a thing." He glanced down at her worried face. "Your brother is worth more than gold."

They hurried back toward Jonah's shed, the night growing colder around them. Jonah's mind raced. They knew where to find Harry now, but stopping a guarded carriage wasn't a simple task. They needed help—people Lockwood couldn't trace back to them.

"We need a plan," Eliza said, voicing his thoughts.

"Yes." Jonah pulled his coat tighter. "But we need more hands," he said, rubbing his jaw. "At least ten men. Strong ones."

Eliza stood in the center of the shed, arms wrapped around herself. "Where would we find men willing to risk themselves against Lockwood's guards?"

"Men with nothing left to lose." Jonah reached for his coat again. "Men who hate Lockwood as much as we do."

"Let me help…"

"No." He cut her off sharply, then softened his tone. "You've been seen with me already. If anyone connects you to whatever happens tomorrow, they'll know exactly who to hunt for."

She squared her shoulders. "I'm not afraid."

"It's not about fear." He hesitated, searching for words. "Harry needs you alive and free."

"So I just sit here while you…"

"I need you to wait." Jonah met her gaze, willing her to understand. "Two hours. If I'm not back by then, make your way to Martha's and stay there."

Eliza's lips pressed into a thin line, but she nodded reluctantly. "Two hours."

Jonah slipped out. The docks would be his best chance. Men worked there who had every reason to hate Lockwood. There would be men whose children or siblings had disappeared into northern mills, men who'd lost wages or positions to Lockwood's schemes.

The Black Anchor tavern stood at the edge of the dockyard, a rough establishment where dockhands drank away their meager earnings. Jonah avoided it most nights because there were too many eyes, too many questions but tonight it might hold exactly what he needed.

He was twenty paces from the tavern when he heard the shouting.

"My son! He's only nine years old, you bastard!"

Jonah ducked into the shadows, watching as the tavern door burst open. A burly man with a full beard flew backward, landing hard on the muddy ground. Behind him stumbled the dock foreman, Walsh, red-faced and unsteady on his feet.

"Get off my property, Riley!" Walsh shouted. "Your boy's gone legal and proper. Nothing to be done about it!"

The bearded man, Riley scrambled to his feet,

lunging for Walsh again only to be intercepted by two larger dockhands who emerged from the tavern.

"You sold him!" Riley roared, struggling against their grip. "You sold my Jamie to that devil Lockwood!"

Walsh straightened his waistcoat, suddenly aware of the small crowd gathering. "Your boy was contracted fair. You signed the papers…"

"When I was three sheets to the wind and you know it!" Riley spat in the mud. "He's all I have left!"

The foreman retreated into the tavern, and the dockhands released Riley with a warning shove. The crowd dispersed quickly, no one wanting to be associated with the man's outburst. Lockwood had too much power over who worked the docks.

Riley stood alone in the mud, his shoulders slumped, and defeat etched into every line of his body.

Perfect.

He waited until the area cleared before approaching. "Bad luck with Walsh," he said quietly.

Riley's head snapped up, eyes narrowing. "What's it to you?"

"I couldn't help overhearing about your son."

"My Jamie." The name sounded wrenched from Riley's throat. "They took him this morning for a seven-year apprenticeship up north." He spat again. "Apprenticeship! They'll work him till he drops."

Jonah moved closer. "When's he being transported?"

Riley looked at him with sudden suspicion. "I don't know. Why?"

"Because I know which one." Jonah lowered his voice further. "And I plan to stop it."

The bigger man stared at him for a long moment. "You're either drunk or mad."

"Neither." Jonah held Riley's gaze steadily. "There's a boy named Harry on that carriage too. His sister came to me for help. But we can't do it alone."

"You're serious." It wasn't a question.

"Dead serious."

Riley ran a hand over his beard, eyes darting around to ensure no one was listening. "What's your stake in this? The girl?"

"Let's just say I have my own score to settle with Lockwood."

Riley studied him, weighing his words. "Even if I believed you could stop that carriage, it's suicide. Lockwood's men are armed."

"So we'll need to be smarter. And we'll need more hands." Jonah crossed his arms. "Do you want your boy back or not?"

"I'd cut off my right arm to get Jamie back."

"I don't need your arm. I need your strength and more men we can trust." Jonah nodded toward the tavern. "Anyone in there who's lost someone to Lockwood's mills?"

Riley's expression darkened. "Half the men in there have lost someone. Question is who's desperate enough to cross Lockwood."

"Find me those men," Jonah said. "I'll wait here."

Riley hesitated only a moment before nodding. "Give me ten minutes."

While Riley disappeared back into the tavern, Jonah positioned himself in the shadows where he could watch both the front and back exits. His hand strayed to his belt where he kept his small knife. It was not much protection if this went sideways, but better than nothing.

True to his word, Riley emerged less than ten minutes later with at least 12 men if he counted correctly following close behind. One was tall and thin with a scar running down one side of his face another was shorter, compact, with forearms like tree trunks.

"This is Jonah Quinn," Riley said by way of introduction. "He's the one I told you about."

The taller man studied Jonah with narrowed

eyes. "I'm Collins. They took my brother three months ago. Haven't heard from him since."

The shorter man nodded curtly. "Harper. My girl was twelve. Lockwood's man said she'd be working as a house servant. Found out later she's at the Blackburn mill."

Jonah assessed them quickly.

"I know exactly which carriage is taking the children north," Jonah said. "And I know where to intercept it, a narrow stretch of road past the Three-Mile marker where there's cover on both sides."

"How many guards?" Collins asked.

"Driver and two or three armed men."

One man snorted. "Just three? Lockwood's getting careless."

"Or confident," Riley added darkly. "No one's ever tried to stop him before."

"So what's the plan?" Collins asked, looking at Jonah expectantly.

Jonah glanced around, making sure they weren't being observed. "Not here. I have a place where we can talk freely."

CHAPTER 9

The cold cut through Eliza's thin shawl like a knife as she crouched behind the thick oak tree. Her breath puffed out in small clouds that disappeared into the dark morning air. The sky was just beginning to lighten, transforming from black to a deep, murky blue.

Jonah and the men were spread out along both sides of the narrow road, hidden in bushes and behind trees. They had been in position for nearly an hour, and Eliza's legs had gone numb from staying still for so long. But the discomfort meant nothing, Harry was all that mattered.

A warm touch on her freezing hand startled her. Jonah had moved silently beside her, his face half-hidden in the shadows.

"Don't worry," he whispered, his fingers briefly squeezing hers. "We'll get him back."

"What if something goes wrong? What if…"

"It won't." His voice was firm, certain. "Riley and his men have nothing left to lose. Lockwood's taken everything from them already."

I have everything to lose, Eliza thought, picturing Harry's thin face. Her entire world was trapped in that carriage.

The distant sound of wheels and hoofbeats silenced their whispers. Eliza pressed herself against the rough bark, heart hammering so loudly she feared it would give away their position.

Two carriages appeared around the bend, moving at a steady pace. The first was smaller with Lockwood's insignia gleaming on its polished door.

"Now," Jonah breathed, and darted from their hiding spot.

The men erupted from the trees like ghosts materializing from the mist. Riley led four men toward the first carriage, while Jonah and the others swarmed the second. The horses reared and whinnied as Riley grabbed their bridles, forcing the vehicle to a jolting stop.

Eliza stayed hidden until the guards poured out of the first carriage, weapons drawn. She counted eight men, more than they'd expected. The air filled with shouts and the sickening sound of wood striking flesh as Lockwood's men clashed with Riley's.

This was her chance. While the guards were occupied, she sprinted toward the second carriage. Its doors were secured with heavy padlocks. Jonah had given her a small iron bar before they'd separated, and she jammed it into the first lock. Her hands shook as she twisted with all her might.

The lock snapped open. She flung the door wide.

"Harry?" she called into the darkness.

Six small faces stared back at her, but none belonged to her brother. The children huddled together on a bench, their wrists bound with rope.

"It's all right," she said, trying to keep her voice steady. "We've come to help you. You're safe now."

She pulled herself into the carriage and used Jonah's knife to cut the nearest child free, a girl no older than seven.

"Can you help the others?" Eliza asked, pressing the knife into the girl's small hand. "I need to find my brother."

The girl nodded, her eyes wide.

Eliza jumped down and ran to the second carriage, her heart in her throat. She could hear fighting behind her, grunts and curses, but couldn't spare a glance. The second lock was sturdier. She jammed the bar into it repeatedly, frustration mounting with each failed attempt.

"Come on, come on," she hissed through gritted teeth.

With a final wrenching twist, the lock broke. She yanked the door open.

"Harry!"

He was there, huddled in the corner, his wrists bound and his face dirty with tear tracks. Ten other children cowered beside him.

"Eliza!" His voice cracked.

She climbed inside and cut his bonds first, her hands trembling so badly she nearly nicked his skin.

"I knew you'd come," he whispered as the rope fell away.

She freed the other children quickly, helping each one climb down from the carriage before turning back to Harry. He launched himself into her arms, his thin body shaking with sobs.

Eliza dropped to her knees in the dirt road, clutching him to her chest. Her own tears spilled over as she pressed kisses to his tangled hair.

"I thought I'd never see you again," Harry cried against her shoulder.

"I'll always find you," she promised, her voice catching. "Always."

She held him at arm's length, quickly checking for injuries. His face was smudged and his clothes filthy, but he seemed unharmed.

Only when she was certain Harry was safe did Eliza look up to assess the battle. Bodies lay on the ground, all wearing Lockwood's colors, she noted with relief. Jonah stood with Riley and three others, his shirt torn and blood trickling from a cut on his cheek. He held a pistol in his hand. The remaining guards were tied to a tree, unconscious.

Their plan had worked. Eliza could scarcely believe it.

"Are you hurt?" Jonah called, striding toward them.

She shook her head, one arm still around Harry's shoulders. "We're fine. All the children are free."

His tense expression softened as he looked at Harry. "You must be the brother I've heard so much about."

Before Harry could respond, the thunder of approaching hoofbeats cut through the dawn air. Eliza turned to see a lone rider galloping toward them, a rifle balanced across the pommel of his saddle.

Silas Grady.

"Get behind me," she ordered Harry, pushing him toward the carriage.

The children who had gathered around her scattered, screaming and diving for cover. Harry clung to her skirts, his fingers digging into the worn fabric.

Grady reined his horse to a stop twenty yards away, his cruel face twisted with fury as he raised his rifle.

Eliza pulled Harry closer as Silas Grady dismounted his horse, rifle in hand. His boots hit the ground with a thud that seemed to echo through her body. The light cast harsh shadows across his face, making his smile look more like a grimace as he approached.

"Well, well," Silas said, his gaze fixed on Jonah. "If it isn't the dead man himself. Jonah Quinn."

Eliza felt her breath catch. Beside her, Harry trembled against her side, but she kept her arm firmly around his shoulders, trying to shield him.

"Grady," Jonah replied.

Silas circled Jonah like a predator, keeping the rifle trained on him. "I knew it was you I spotted at the docks. The moment I saw you skulking around, something didn't sit right." He tapped the side of his head. "I never forget a face, especially one that's supposed to be rotting at the bottom of the Thames."

Riley and the other men had gone still, watching the exchange with wary eyes.

"How's life been treating you since you fixed your death?" Silas continued, his voice mockingly casual. "Living in squalor, I see. Working the docks like common trash. All that potential wasted."

Jonah's jaw tightened. "Better than being Lockwood's lapdog."

Silas's smile vanished. He jabbed the rifle barrel into Jonah's chest. "You still have a death to pay to Lockwood. Running didn't clear your debt."

"I didn't steal anything," Jonah said, not flinching from the barrel. "You framed me, and we both know it."

Silas laughed, a hollow sound. "There's no way you can prove that. No one would believe a dead thief over me."

"I don't care about proving anything," Jonah replied, his gaze unwavering. "But I'm not letting you take these children."

As if on cue, Riley and the other men moved forward, forming a protective curve around Jonah. The children huddled near the carriages, some clutching each other's hands.

Silas looked around at the men surrounding Jonah and laughed again, louder this time. The sound sent chills down Eliza's spine.

"Did you really think I'd come alone?" He raised his hand and gave a sharp whistle.

From the trees and brush on both sides of the road, men emerged, at least fifteen of them, armed with clubs. Lockwood's men. They must have been trailing the carriages at a distance, ready for any trouble.

"Do you think I wouldn't have reinforcements?" Silas sneered.

Eliza's heart sank. They were outnumbered. She tightened her grip on Harry, her mind racing for an escape route.

"Run," she whispered to him. "Take the other children and hide in the woods."

Harry shook his head, clinging to her. "I won't leave you."

"You must," she insisted. "I'll find you, I promise."

Before Harry could protest further, the clash began. Riley was the first to move, charging at Silas with a roar. The other men followed, meeting Lockwood's thugs head-on.

Eliza shoved Harry toward the trees. "Go! Now!"

This time he obeyed, gathering the nearest children and darting into the undergrowth. Eliza turned back to the chaos, scanning desperately for Jonah. She spotted him grappling with one of Lockwood's men, his movements swift and precise despite the night's exertions.

The fight was brutal and swift. Eliza pressed herself against the carriage, watching in horror as men fell on both sides. Riley took down two of Lockwood's thugs before a third caught him across the back with a club. The men fought like a man possessed.

But Lockwood's men had numbers on their side. One by one, Riley's men went down, overwhelmed by the sheer force against them. Only Jonah and two others remained standing, surrounded by a circle of Lockwood's men.

Silas had retreated to the edge of the fight, watching with satisfaction as his men gained the upper hand. When he saw that only Jonah and two others still fought, he raised his rifle again.

"Enough playing," he called out. "Finish them!"

Eliza saw him take aim at Jonah and acted without thinking. She snatched a rock from the ground and hurled it with all her might. It struck Silas's shoulder, throwing off his aim as he fired.

The shot went wide, missing Jonah by inches.

Silas whirled toward her, his face contorted with fury. Before he could raise the rifle again, Riley's men, those who had been knocked down but not out, surged forward with renewed strength.

Silas fired wildly into the crowd. Three sharp cracks split the air.

Jonah staggered backward, clutching his side. Two other men fell, one of Riley's friends and one of Lockwood's thugs.

"Jonah!" Eliza screamed.

The sight of Jonah wounded seemed to ignite something in the remaining men. They converged on Silas, tackling him to the ground. The rifle flew from his hands, skidding across the dirt.

Eliza ran to Jonah, who had slumped against the carriage wheel. Blood seeped between his fingers where he pressed them to his side.

"Let me see," she demanded, kneeling beside him. Her hands shook as she gently pulled his away from the wound.

The bullet had torn through his jacket and shirt, leaving a deep groove along his ribs. It was bleeding heavily, but hadn't penetrated his chest.

"It's not deep," she told him, relief making her voice unsteady. "The bullet just grazed you."

Jonah's face was pale, but he managed a tight smile. "Lucky, then."

Behind them, Silas's cries had diminished to whimpers as the men continued their assault. When they finally stepped back, Silas Grady lay motionless in the dirt, his face unrecognizable beneath blood and bruises.

"Is he dead?" Eliza asked, still pressing her wadded shawl against Jonah's side.

Riley limped over to check. "No," he said after a moment. "Unfortunately for him, he's still breathing."

"Tie him up," Jonah instructed through gritted teeth. "Him and any others still conscious. We'll decide what to do with them later."

Eliza turned her attention back to Jonah's wound. She tore a strip from her petticoat to create a proper bandage, wrapping it tightly around his ribs.

"You're going to need stitches," she told him as she secured the knot.

"I've had worse," he replied, though his breathing was shallow.

"Harry," she suddenly remembered, her head jerking up. "Harry!" she called toward the trees.

For a terrible moment, there was no response.

Then the undergrowth rustled, and Harry came out, leading the other children. His face brightened when he saw her, but fell again when he noticed Jonah's condition.

"Is he going to die?" Harry asked in a small voice.

"No," Eliza said firmly, helping Jonah to sit up straighter. "He's going to be just fine. We all are."

Jonah reached out with his good arm and ruffled Harry's hair. "It would take more than Silas Grady to finish me off, lad."

Harry's smile returned.

Riley approached them, his own face bloodied from the fight. "We need to move quickly. More of Lockwood's men might come looking when these don't return."

Eliza nodded. "Can you stand?" she asked Jonah.

With her help and Riley's, Jonah got to his feet, wincing as the movement pulled at his wound.

"What now?" Eliza asked, looking around at the aftermath of the battle—wounded men, destroyed carriages, and the children watching with wide, frightened eyes.

"We get these children home," Jonah said. "And then..." He paused and then he slumped.

CHAPTER 10

The brightness slipped through the window cracks like thieves, lancing into Jonah's eyes. A dull throb followed immediately along his side that sharpened to fire when he tried to sit up. His memory returned in fragmented flashes: Grady's gun, the children escaping, Eliza's horrified face as she pressed against his bleeding side.

Eliza.

He forced his eyes fully open, blinking away the fog of what must have been laudanum-induced sleep. The room around him was unfamiliar. It was small but clean, with yellowed wallpaper and a faded rug. Not a hospital ward, certainly not his shed, and leagues away from the prison cell he'd half-expected to wake in.

His gaze settled on the corner of the room where two figures were slumped together in a narrow chair. Eliza sat with her head fallen to one side, dark hair spilling over her shoulder. Harry was curled impossibly small against her, his face half-buried in her shawl, one little hand clutching his sister's sleeve even in sleep.

Something unfamiliar and dangerously warm flooded Jonah's chest. He'd spent five years avoiding attachments, cutting every connection that might lead Lockwood's men to him. Five years of careful isolation. And now, watching Eliza and Harry breathe in unison, he felt like he'd stumbled into something he never knew he was missing.

Like he belonged somewhere. To someone.

The thought terrified him more than Grady's rifle had.

A floorboard creaked as he shifted, and Eliza's eyes flew open. For a split second, naked relief washed across her face before she composed herself.

"You're awake," she whispered, carefully extracting herself from Harry, who mumbled something incomprehensible before settling back into sleep. "How bad is it?"

"I've had worse." The lie came automatically,

though in truth he couldn't remember pain quite like this.

Eliza rolled her eyes. "Of course you have." She crossed to his bedside and pressed her palm against his forehead, her touch cool and efficient. "Your fever broke last night. Martha said that was a good sign."

"Martha?"

"Hughes. The seamstress. This is her house." Eliza straightened his blanket with unnecessary attention. "After everything at Highgate, we couldn't take you to a doctor, not with Lockwood's influence. Martha has experience with... injuries."

"Smart," he croaked, his throat sandpaper-dry.

Eliza poured water from a pitcher beside the bed, supporting his head as he drank. The simple movement made his side scream in protest.

"How long have I been out?"

"Three days. You lost blood, then the fever came." Her voice was matter-of-fact, but the shadows under her eyes told a different story. "Martha called a nurse and she stitched you up. The bullet only grazed your side, but it was deep enough."

"And the children?"

"All safe. Riley and the men got them back to

their families... Word's spreading about what Lockwood was doing and people are talking."

Before Jonah could respond, the door opened. Martha Hughes entered, her practical skirts swishing as she moved. Jonah had only seen her briefly before, during his one visit to her shop, but he recognized the no-nonsense set of her mouth.

"Our patient's decided to join the living, then." She approached the bed and checked his bandages. "Clean wound, healing well. You're lucky, Mr. Quinn. An inch deeper and we'd be selecting a coffin instead of changing dressings."

"Thank you for..."

"Save it." Martha cut him off. "I'm just evening the score." She glanced at Harry, still sleeping in the chair. "That boy hasn't left your side except when we made him eat. Thinks you hung the moon after you saved him."

Jonah couldn't look at Harry. The devotion felt unearned, uncomfortable.

Martha straightened, her expression shifting to something more serious. "There's someone here to see you. Has been waiting since yesterday."

Eliza stiffened. "You didn't say..."

"Didn't want to worry you until he was awake." Martha nodded toward Jonah. "It's Inspector

Holloway from the Bow Street Runners. He's investigating Augustus Lockwood."

Jonah's pulse quickened, his pain momentarily forgotten. The Runners were London's closest thing to actual police. They were magistrate-appointed men who investigated serious crimes. If they were looking into Lockwood...

"He says he needs information," Martha continued. "Told him you'd been shot by Lockwood's man, but not why. Figured that was your story to tell."

Jonah looked at Eliza, whose face had gone pale.

"Do you trust this inspector?" he asked.

"Never met him before," Martha replied. "But he showed proper credentials. And he's not alone. He brought a secretary to take notes." She paused. "He mentioned your name specifically, Jonah Quinn."

"I'll send him away if you want," Martha offered, reading his expression.

Jonah thought of the children packed into Lockwood's carriages. Of Eliza's desperation to save Harry. Of how many others had been sold to northern mills over the years.

"No," he said finally. "I'll talk to him."

Martha nodded once and left. Eliza moved closer to the bed.

"Are you sure?" she whispered. "If they know who you are..."

"I'm already discovered." He tried for a smile but suspected it came out as a grimace. "Might as well make it count."

She squeezed his hand quickly, then withdrew as the door opened again.

Inspector Holloway was a tall man with a trim mustache and intelligent eyes that missed nothing as he entered. His clothes were well-made but not flashy—the attire of a man who needed to move between social classes without drawing attention. Behind him came a younger man carrying a leather portfolio.

"Mr. Quinn." Holloway nodded at Jonah. "I'm glad to see you recovering. I understand there was quite a confrontation at Highgate."

"You could say that." Jonah carefully shifted to sit straighter, unwilling to look weak.

The inspector pulled a chair beside the bed. "I've been investigating Augustus Lockwood for some months now for child labor violations, fraud, blackmail..." He leaned forward. "But witnesses have a habit of disappearing. Or recanting their statements after visits from a man named Silas Grady."

At Grady's name, Harry stirred in the corner. Eliza immediately went to him, murmuring softly.

"What happened to Grady?" Jonah asked.

"He's currently enjoying the hospitality of Newgate Prison," Holloway said with a hint of satisfaction. "Found unconscious at Highgate with several other men, all tied to trees. Was an interesting scene."

Relief loosened something in Jonah's chest. At least Grady wouldn't be hunting them while he recovered.

"I understand you were once employed by Lockwood," the inspector continued. "As a cooper's apprentice. Until you supposedly drowned in the Thames five years ago after being accused of theft."

"I didn't steal anything." The words burst out with more force than Jonah intended.

"I believe you." Holloway nodded to his secretary, who began writing. "That's why I'm here. I need your testimony on everything Lockwood did, everything you know. The children were just the latest in his schemes."

Jonah glanced at Eliza, who gave him a small nod of encouragement.

"You think you can actually bring him down?"

Doubt colored his voice. "Men like Lockwood don't fall."

"They do with enough evidence." Holloway's gaze was steady. "And I believe you have pieces I need."

Jonah took a breath, ignoring the pain that shot through his side.

"Five years ago, I was finishing my apprenticeship under Master Cooper Jenkins when Lockwood bought his shop. Jenkins was old, his hands weren't steady anymore, but he taught me everything." The memory was still bitter. "Lockwood brought in a shipment of French brandy—expensive stuff. When three casks went missing, he accused me of stealing them."

"Did you?"

"No. I'd worked four years for that position. I wouldn't risk it for a few bottles." Jonah's hands clenched in the blankets. "Lockwood's real target was Jenkins. The old man owned prime property near the docks that Lockwood wanted. The accusation against me was leverage."

Holloway's secretary's pen scratched across the paper.

"Jenkins testified that I couldn't have taken the brandy since I was with him when it supposedly disappeared. But Lockwood had already paid off the magistrate." Jonah's mouth twisted. "I was sentenced to transportation. Seven years in Australia."

"But you jumped into the Thames instead," Holloway finished.

"From the prison barge. Guards were drunk and the current was strong. Everyone assumed I drowned." Jonah shrugged. "Seemed better than letting Lockwood win."

"And Jenkins?"

"Sold to Lockwood for half its worth after I 'died.' Died himself six months later."

Holloway nodded grimly. "We've found similar patterns with other businesses Lockwood acquired. False accusations, mysterious accidents."

"There's more," Jonah said, his voice strengthening. "During the past five years on the docks, I've kept my ears open. Talk to Foreman Miller at Warehouse Four, he has a private ledger of all Lockwood's 'unofficial shipments.' Children, smuggled goods."

The secretary's pen flew across the page.

"Miller won't talk willingly," Jonah warned.

"We have ways of encouraging cooperation," Holloway said dryly.

"There's also Morgan at the Hound and Crown. He's an information broker and be knows everyone Lockwood's threatened or bribed."

"We're familiar with Morgan," Holloway said with distaste.

"And the children from the carriages," Eliza interjected suddenly. All eyes turned toward her. "They can testify to being kidnapped. Harry can tell you how Grady took him to pay my father's debt."

"Will it be enough?" Jonah asked. "Lockwood has powerful friends."

"Had," Holloway corrected. "His recent activities have made him a liability to his social circle. Especially after the Highgate incident became public knowledge." He leaned forward. "Which brings me to another matter. The attack on Lockwood's carriages."

"Technically, interfering with property transport is a crime," Holloway said slowly. "However, as the 'property' in question was illegally obtained children..." He spread his hands. "No charges will be pressed against the... concerned citizens who intervened."

The relief was immediate. Jonah hadn't realized how worried he'd been about Riley and the others.

"As for your own situation, Mr. Quinn," Holloway continued, "the original theft charges against you are being reviewed. With Jenkins' testimony on record and evidence of Lockwood's pattern of fraudulent accusations, I expect they'll be dismissed entirely."

Jonah stared at him. "You mean I'm not a fugitive anymore?"

"Not for the theft, certainly." A slight smile touched Holloway's mouth. "Though I'd advise against faking your own death again in the future. Creates a nightmare of paperwork."

A strange lightness filled Jonah's chest that had nothing to do with his wound. Five years of looking over his shoulder, of living in shadows. Over.

"I'll need your formal statement once you're well enough to come to the magistrate's office," Holloway said, rising. "A week, perhaps?"

"Yes. Thank you."

The inspector nodded farewell and left with his secretary, Martha showing them out. In the sudden quiet, Jonah found himself looking at Eliza, whose eyes shone with something he couldn't quite name.

"Did you hear that?" she asked softly. "You're free."

Free. The word felt foreign, impossible.

Harry scrambled up from his chair and approached the bed cautiously. "Does that mean you don't have to hide anymore? Or run away?"

"I suppose it does." The realization was still sinking in.

"Good." Harry nodded with the decisive certainty of a child. "Because I still owe you for saving me, and Eliza says debts should always be paid."

Despite the pain, the years of fear, the uncertainty still ahead—Jonah felt laughter bubble up in his chest. It hurt his side, but he couldn't stop it.

"Well," he said, looking from Harry to Eliza, whose smile could have lit all of London, "I guess I'll have to stick around, then."

CHAPTER 11

Eliza stood before the tiny mirror propped against the wall of their new room, attempting to tame her hair into something presentable. The room might not be much bigger than their previous one, but it was cleaner, warmer, and, most importantly, nowhere near their old building. After everything with Lockwood, a fresh start had seemed essential.

"You're going to wear a hole in that brush if you keep at it," Harry commented from his seat on the edge of the bed, swinging his legs back and forth. His cheeks had more color these days, and his cough had improved considerably with proper medicine and regular meals.

Eliza shot him a look. "I just want to look decent, that's all."

"Decent? You've tried on three dresses already!" Harry grinned, clearly enjoying her flustered state. "The blue one looked fine. And the brown one. And even the gray one."

She ignored him and returned to the green dress she'd finally settled on, one Martha had helped her make from mill ends that would have otherwise been discarded. The fabric was soft, with tiny yellow flowers embroidered along the hem.

"He won't care what you're wearing anyway," Harry continued, flopping back onto the bed. "He looks at you the same way no matter what you have on."

"And how's that?" Eliza asked, despite herself.

"Like you're the only person in the room." Harry made exaggerated swooning motions. "It's disgusting, really."

Heat rushed to Eliza's cheeks. "That's quite enough out of you."

"You're acting like you've never spent time with him before," Harry pointed out. "You've seen him every day for weeks."

"That was different," she muttered, smoothing her hands over the dress. "That was while he was recovering. And while everything with Lockwood was being sorted. This is..."

"A proper courting," Harry finished, in a passable imitation of Martha's voice that made Eliza laugh despite her nerves.

It had been a month since everything changed. A month since Jonah's testimony, along with evidence from the ledgers, the rescued children, and several other witnesses, had brought Augustus Lockwood's empire crashing down. The self-important merchant now sat in Newgate awaiting trial, his properties seized, his accounts frozen. Silas Grady had been shipped off to Australia on the very transport ship he'd once threatened others with.

And Thomas Tate? Eliza hadn't seen him since that terrible day. She'd heard he'd left London entirely, heading north to try his luck in Manchester. Sometimes guilt pricked at her for the harsh words she'd spoken to him, but she couldn't bring herself to regret them. He'd needed to hear the truth.

A knock at the door made Eliza jump.

"He's here!" Harry shouted, bouncing off the bed and racing to the door before Eliza could stop him.

"Harry, wait!" But he'd already thrown the door open.

Jonah Quinn stood in the doorway, looking remarkably different from the wary dockworker she'd first met. His hair was neatly trimmed, his face clean-shaven, and his clothes, while still simple, were well-kept. The biggest change, though, was in his eyes. It was no longer constantly scanning for threats, they now held a steadiness that made something flutter in Eliza's chest.

"Good morning," he said, his gaze finding hers immediately before shifting to Harry. "And how are you today, Master Tate?"

"Hungry," Harry replied promptly, making Jonah laugh.

"What a coincidence." Jonah reached into his pocket and produced a small brown paper bag. "I happened to pass by Mrs. Wilson's bakery on my way here."

Harry's eyes widened as he peered inside the bag. "Cinnamon buns!"

"Just the one," Jonah clarified with a smile. "Best save the rest of your appetite for later."

Eliza approached them, suddenly feeling shy despite having spent countless hours in Jonah's company over the past month—first helping care for his wound, then assisting Inspector Holloway with building the case against Lockwood.

"You didn't have to bring anything," she said.

"I wanted to." His eyes traveled over her dress. "You look beautiful."

The simple compliment, delivered without flourish, warmed her far more than elaborate flattery would have.

"When are you two getting married?" Harry asked around a mouthful of cinnamon bun.

"Harry!" Eliza gasped, mortification washing over her.

But Jonah just laughed, his eyes crinkling at the corners. "Immediately, if your sister permits it."

"Jonah!" Now her face was definitely flaming.

"What?" he asked innocently. "I'm merely answering the question."

Harry looked between them with a satisfied expression. "Good. I like having you around."

"I like being around," Jonah replied, his eyes never leaving Eliza's.

She cleared her throat, desperate to change the subject before she spontaneously combusted from embarrassment. "We should go. I told Martha I'd stop by the shop later to pick up some thread."

"Of course," Jonah agreed, still looking far too amused.

Eliza turned to Harry. "You'll be good for Mrs.

Cooper downstairs?"

Harry nodded, already halfway through his treat. "I'm helping with the baby. She says I'm a natural."

"Just don't teach him any of your bad habits," Eliza warned, ruffling his hair as she reached for her shawl.

"Like what?" Harry asked innocently.

"Like asking improper questions," she replied pointedly, making Jonah chuckle again.

They left Harry happily finishing his cinnamon bun and descended the narrow stairs to the street below. The spring air held a hint of warmth, a welcome change from the bitter cold that had gripped London during their confrontation with Lockwood.

"He seems much better," Jonah observed as they walked side by side.

"The cough's almost gone," Eliza confirmed. "Dr. Bennett says his lungs sound clearer every week."

"And how are you?" Jonah asked, his voice softening. "Really."

Eliza considered the question. "Busy. The work with Martha keeps my hands full, and taking care of Harry..." She paused. "But good. For the first time in a long while, I'm not terrified about tomorrow."

Jonah nodded in understanding. "And your

father?"

"Nothing," she answered, a slight tightness in her voice. "Which is probably for the best. I said things I can't take back."

"He earned every word," Jonah said firmly.

"Perhaps. But he wasn't always..." She trailed off, not wanting to dwell on Thomas today. "What about you? How's the new position?"

The hint of pride in Jonah's expression made her smile. Inspector Holloway, impressed by Jonah's testimony and knowledge of the docks, had recommended him for a position with the Customs Office —a respectable job with steady pay and no backbreaking labor.

"Still learning all the paperwork," Jonah admitted. "But it's good. Honest work, and I don't have to keep looking over my shoulder."

They wandered through the streets, heading toward the river. London bustled around them, indifferent to the small revolution that had occurred in its underbelly.

"Ice cream?" Jonah suggested as they passed a vendor with a small cart.

Eliza raised her eyebrows. "At this hour?"

"Why not? We're celebrating, aren't we?"

"And what are we celebrating?" she asked, though

she couldn't keep the smile from her lips.

"Being alive. Being free." He looked at her meaningfully. "Being together."

Something in his direct gaze made her feel both vulnerable and brave. "Yes to the ice cream, then."

They sat on a bench overlooking the Thames, licking their treats and watching boats pass. The river that had once been Jonah's salvation, the water that had helped him escape Lockwood's clutches, now seemed benign in the spring sunlight.

"You know," Jonah said thoughtfully, "I never thought I'd have this."

"Ice cream on a Tuesday morning?" Eliza teased.

He smiled but shook his head. "A normal life. After I jumped in the river that night, I thought I'd always be running, always looking over my shoulder." He paused. "I never planned to care about anyone. It seemed too dangerous."

The simple confession touched something deep inside her. "I know what you mean. After Mother died and Father... changed, I decided it was safer not to count on anyone but myself."

"And Harry," Jonah added.

"And Harry," she agreed. "But even with him, I was so focused on survival that I couldn't see past the next day, the next shilling, the next meal."

They were quiet for a moment, finishing their ice cream. A ship's horn sounded in the distance.

"Do you miss it?" Eliza asked suddenly. "The docks, I mean."

Jonah considered this. "The work? No. But there's a certain freedom in having nothing to lose." He glanced at her. "Though I've discovered having something to live for is better."

The warmth in his gray eyes made her heart skip. She'd never been one for flowery sentiments or grand gestures, but the honest simplicity of his words moved her more than poetry ever could.

"What are you thinking?" he asked, noticing her expression.

Eliza laughed, suddenly feeling lighter than she had in years. "That Harry was right. This is our first proper outing together, and yet it feels like we've known each other forever."

"We have survived a shooting, brought down a corrupt merchant, and rescued more than a dozen children together," Jonah pointed out wryly. "That does tend to accelerate things."

"When you put it that way..."

They continued their walk, ambling along the embankment without any particular destination. Jonah told her stories about his new colleagues at the Customs House, and Eliza shared gossip from Martha's shop, including the news that Martha herself might be sweet on Inspector Holloway after his frequent visits to interview the staff.

"I've never laughed this much," Eliza realized aloud as they paused to watch a street performer juggling colored balls.

Jonah looked at her with surprise. "Never?"

"Not since I was a child, at least." She considered this. "I didn't have much cause for it, I suppose."

"Then I'll have to make sure you have reason to laugh every day from now on," he said, with such straightforward conviction that she believed him.

As they turned back toward Spitalfields, the afternoon sun warm on their faces, Eliza felt a contentment she'd almost forgotten was possible. For the first time in years, she wasn't running from something or striving desperately toward something else. She was simply here, walking beside a man who looked at her like she was the most fascinating person he'd ever met.

"Eliza," Jonah said, his voice suddenly serious as they reached a quieter street. "I meant what I said to Harry earlier."

She blinked at him, momentarily confused before

remembering Harry's mortifying question about marriage.

"Oh! I know you were just being kind…"

"No," he interrupted, stopping and turning to face her fully. "I wasn't just being kind. I know it's fast, by normal standards. But nothing about us has followed the usual path, has it?"

Her heart pounded uncomfortably in her chest. "Jonah…"

"I'm not asking today," he clarified quickly. "But I want you to know that's where my thoughts lie. When I thought I might die from that gunshot, all I could think about was you and Harry, and the future I wanted with both of you."

Eliza felt as though she couldn't quite catch her breath. "I thought the same," she admitted quietly. "When I saw you fall, I realized I couldn't lose you."

The smile that spread across his face was like sunrise breaking over the horizon. Slowly, giving her plenty of time to step away if she chose, he leaned down and pressed his lips to hers in a gentle kiss that promised both passion and tenderness.

When they broke apart, she couldn't help but laugh at the dazed look on his face.

"What's so funny?" he asked.

"Nothing," she said, still smiling. "I'm just happy."

Printed in Great Britain
by Amazon